Novel set in Colorado   Mother's Day, 1981

.75

To Mother —
    That you may share the
work of my friend, Sheila.
                    Love,
                    Susan

IN ROOMS OF FALLING RAIN

by

Sheila Nickerson

Thorp Springs Press

Children, the threshold of the storm
has slid beneath your muddy shoes;
wet and beguiled, you stand among
the mansions you may choose
out of a bigger house than yours,
whose lawfulness endures,
Its soggy documents retain
your rights in rooms of falling rain.

—Elizabeth Bishop

Cover Drawing by Amelia Gianelli

Nickerson, Sheila.
    In rooms of falling rain.

    I. Title.
PZ4.N633In   [PS3564.I288]   813'.5'4   76-28466

ISBN: 0-914476-59-9 paper
ISBN: 0-914476-56-4 library binding

THORP SPRINGS PRESS
2311-C Woolsey Street
Berkeley, California 94705

PART I

I

Harriet tripped over the chair as she hurried for the phone. The ringing would wake the children and they would cry with fright again. John's voice cracked through the dark and the wind. "I'll be down here," he said. "It's something of a disaster with three major fires going."

"Where?"

"Two to the northeast, one up in Harebell Canyon."

"Harebell Canyon. That's right up the road. Is there any danger here?"

"No, I'd come right home if there were."

Only then did she become aware of the smoke standing in the room like a living thing, something growing and taking shape. Shaking herself awake, she remembered. After the lights went out John left to get more candles. Now he was down at the Mayor's office. *I was something more than wind.*

She couldn't find the hook for the receiver, even when she held the phone up to the window where some weak moonlight played. How clumsy, she thought, rattling the black dead thing on the table. How clumsy it all was, falling over things in this sudden dark. She felt her way through the hall and down the living room to the large window at the far end. It was then that she saw it, the high pink sheet stretched against the front range. It must have been there, growing, all the while she slept here alone with the children and the old deaf dog.

The wind, hours old now, threw itself repeatedly against the house. The furniture braced against the terrace doors squeaked on the floor. The awning frame groaned and the screen door in back crashed rhythmically against the clapboard.

3

With her eyes adjusted to the dark, Harriet picked out specific objects in the yard. The small crabapple bent grotesquely. Several cardboard boxes danced like leaves. A board lay across the iris bed. Spring was a long way off. And she had never put away the garden tools. Finally she looked up, above the yard, to face it more thoroughly.

The mesa just below the rock face burned red. High bright clouds radiating from it illuminated miles of the foothills. Silhouettes of trees, houses, and poles played in and out of the gusting smoke. Searchlights arced over the redness, bisecting it. They sky was curiously gentle, ribbons of cloud teasing the solemn moon face.

It couldn't really be happening. Only in Australia, or California, at worst, could such a thing happen. Margot and Jeff were right there asleep in the next room, and a hundred other babies close by in Sand Creek that night.

The wind struck the house like a giant fist. Harriet recoiled from the window. A metallic crash reverberated as the gust died, probably a garbage can from the alley. She should go out to lock the garage doors. John would if he were home.

If only the children wouldn't wake up. Margot, at three, had been rigid with fright as the wind slammed against the house and the lights flickered on and off. Even the baby had been strangely restless. Harriet had tried hard to make light of it. The wind was only like the wicked wolf saying, "I'll huff and I'll puff and I'll blow your house down."

After many nursery rhymes Margot had fallen asleep, and in the next room, the baby. The lights died, as if, suddenly, exhausted. John prowled through the house becoming more nervous with each blast. The batteries were weak, and the candles weren't enough. After flinging himself next to her on the bed, he had gotten up, changed his clothes as if for work and left. Alone in the dark she had fallen asleep. She could not remember dreaming, though it seemed impossible to lie blank at such a time.

With a flashlight she checked on the children. They were motionless, huddled in their separate private noises of sleep. Next, the garage. In a raincoat and boots, the first thing she could find in the dark closet, she opened the front door. From the porch the night seemed serene. Wisps of cloud still played about the moon. Then a tearing gust bent down the trees in front of her. Still protected by the west wing, she didn't feel it as they did, bowing wildly and long to the east. She broke, running, to the garage. The door was down and locked. Harriet flattened herself against the garage door as the wind threw itself to the east. She watched its ghost stream rush by her carrying branches and paper. Voices from the burning mesa threaded the debris. The gust quieted and she ran to the porch. A few seconds, or minutes, might remain before the next blast. All down the street flashlights skipped like fireflies. But this was the West where fireflies were unknown and the balmy thick nights that fireflies inhabit. Directly across from her Old Oscar Dobbins was hosing down his house. Even the ripping gusts didn't dissuade him from his methodical job. That could hardly help, she thought, in a wind like this. Nobody else was hosing. In January most hoses would be put away. Theirs was; nor would she know where to look for it.

Further down the street a number of cars with headlights on were parked. Sightseers. People waiting in the dark for something terrible to happen.

Far out to the northeast, near the airport, a red glow hovered on the horizon. Immediately below, at the foot of Canyon Street, houselights blazed in one small patch, a curious night-blooming garden.

Inside Harriet sat by the front window, next to the telephone, watching Mr. Dobbins hose down his house. Her eyes burned with smoke, but there was nothing to be done. She wanted to go back to the garage, open the door, get inside the car and listen to the radio, but the children might wake up when she was gone. There was no telling where John might be by now, or if he would let her know of real danger.

Margot called out as the house shook with a blast of wind. Then both were silent. Harriet knew she had to look again out the south window at the fire. She threaded the living room. The flashlight batteries had to be saved. Candles were dangerous, especially now. Her eyes were already adjusted to the dark. Before she got to the end of the room she saw the glow, definitely further down the slope than before. Huge searchlights based at the weather station bisected it. The new houses up at Needle's Eye, those triangles and spirals of frivolity, would be as vulnerable as any fir tree.

When they bought here on Canyon Street, they had not thought of vulnerability. The mountains, though awesome, were at least two miles away and had seemed, at first sight, a protective wall. The neatly yarded neighborhood could have stood anywhere in the country, could have appeared in any magazine. They should have thought. Already, in a year, they had experienced hail and flood, lightning and wind beyond comprehension. Now this.

Margot called again. This time she was awake. The darkness could not disguise the largeness of her eyes. She didn't question. She only looked at her mother for assurance. Harriet sighed and sat down beside her. How small she looked in the twin bed she had just moved into from the crib. How small in a room all her own.

"It's only the wind, sweetheart, doing his job. Do you remember the story of Frances the Badger who asked her father why the curtains blew?"

Margot pushed back the covers to climb onto Harriet's lap. "Where have the lights gone?" she asked.

Hariet couldn't remember reading any story about electricity going off; she wouldn't try to explain it in scientific terms, as John would.

As Margot nestled against her, waiting, a sudden torrent of wind hit the house with the force of an explosion. A violent smash came from the south living room window, followed by the sound of splintering glass. She held back a scream. Alone in the dark with the children, she would be crushed in the collapse of the house. A wave of smoky air washed over her.

"Mommy!"

Margot, shocked beyond crying, stared at the door to the living room through which the wind poured. They both stared.

The whole window—half the wall—was gone. She didn't have to go see. The west wall, with its French doors to the terrace, would go next. Only the east and north sides of the house were solid. The house would blow down and they would be swept away.

"Margot. It's all right. The wind just got very strong and knocked the window in, that's all. Silly wind."

The child didn't respond as she usually did with the word "silly," her omnibus word of rebuke.

"I'll call Daddy at the office and ask him to come home to fix it."

6

She heard her voice, as if from somebody else, slithering through the room, looking for a resting place. Wraith. Wraiths all tonight, perched on the foot of the giant mountains at the end of the plains. Nebraska, Colorado—they had just been terms of geography until such a short time ago. Now they were the wind pulling down her walls. She wanted to be home, but home was gone. There was no home.

Harriet handed the flashlight, with its precious batteries, to the child and walked through the baby's room back to the north end of the living room, to the phone table. No longer thinking of the dark she dialed John's office at the Municipal Building. Only after waiting some time did she realize the phone was dead. She was not surprised. Tonight everything would blow away and burn but essence. It was Biblical and inevitable; she could not quite remember how it went.

Air flowed around her, still strangely warm. Before the electricity went off the temperature was over 60°—a portent they should have noted.

Margot was calling, alone too long in the dark of her new and solitary bed. She had begged to have the baby stay with her in her room.

Now Jeff, too, was awake, reaching up to the bars of his crib. She wished she could hold him to her breast but she had weaned him a week ago. There was only a hard lump where there had been milk. She would have to go to the kitchen to get him a bottle—a long trip from Margot in bed with the gaping headboard like a face.

While they both cried she made her way to the kitchen, tripping across old Betsy, the deaf spaniel asleep on the threshold. The room was lighted by the fire, the enamel throwing off a pinkness of its own. When opened, the refrigerator stayed dark, nor was there any need to shut it. How distant the ritual of the morning seemed—the careful opening and shutting, the turning on and off, the putting in and the taking out.

With the baby on her lap she sat on Margot's bed. They would tell all their friends in the woods about it. After, they would have a party.

"Will Daddy be here?" she asked.

"Of course, when he's finished." Eventually he would have to come home, if only for breakfast.

7

The ripping of wood cut through the story. The Russian olive next door at the Fergusons' had fallen. She knew the silver tangle of willowy branches without seeing it, the net that had caught up the storm and exploded with it. At least it was small, nothing to fall across the roof. The mountain weather allowed few trees to grow roof-tall. And before the settlers there had been none except for the twisted cottonwoods snaking the course of the creeks, billowing with their snowy seed pods in June. Flying over the plains she had watched them, puffs of green on the empty summer map. How much emptier it must have been here at the time of the Indians, and how much simpler for the wind.

II

Out on Highway 7 running parallel with the mountains, Dick Eddy slammed on the brakes and tried to turn the wheel west, into the wind. His truck shuddered and rolled as he fought for control of it. Oh God, this is it, he thought as a coldness boxed him. The truck took one last swerve and crashed over the shoulder, down the sandy embankment many feet to the grassland below. Tumbleweed followed him until the wind broke and the road was empty. Clouds like a gossamer scarf pulled across the moon.

On the south end of Sand Creek a herd of horses waiting to be traded panicked in their small corral. Galloping from corner to corner in frenzied diagonals, they churned up hard clods which struck against each other and the fence. The leader, a palomino, finally broke through the fence by charging against it. With blood dripping down his front legs he led his herd north by the nearest road, clattering past the darkened houses where candles flickered and faces bobbed. A mare and foal, unable to keep up with the others, dropped behind.

In a large Victorian house in central Sand Creek, Jessie Findlay huddled in her immense bed. A child of the wind, now grown old in it, she considered it part of her fabric. The first-remembered blizzards of Nebraska, the dust-bowl days of eastern Colorado, and finally the crying old age of Sand Creek were all part of it. Even the day Henry died was marked by wind, wind which howled in with snow almost a year ago. She thought of his soul, anchored to bright space. It had been a crashing day of light and dark, a wild day for the uninitiated to slip into like that. Now the house shuddered, its loose parts ripping. How had he found his way? Whatever damage there was would have to stay unfixed. The house would grow very old that night.

Bob Dowdey looked out his front window to see the old couch lifted off the porch and hurled down the sloping lawn toward the street. As he stepped back a rock crashed through the glass and landed by his feet. Behind him Marcia screamed. She would have to take the children down to the basement until it was over. The dog howled.

It would happen this night of all nights, Anne Cox thought in her living room so suddenly emptied of guests. Their housewarming. It could only be an omen. They had put far too much into the place. The bills were frightening. Now Doug said they would be lucky if the concrete wall didn't hurl into the west side of the house and smash the whole thing. No matter what happened, they couldn't put on another party like this for a long time. The shrimp alone had cost a staggering amount. The Evanses hadn't even gotten here at all, nor the Whitesides. And now Melanie was screaming.

Up in Harebell Canyon the first of the looters had arrived and were forcing their way into the empty summer houses. With the fire contained only by a macadam road upwind, they worked with the heat of the flames on their faces. Their expressions were contorted by light and shadow, their silhouettes part of the frenzied dance of the night.

Far away in Chicago, Houston, and hamlets in between, the owners slept oblivious.

From the old wooden *Courier* building, Clyde Hansen looked out on the storm with dismay. A native of Sand Creek, a man who thought he experienced everything in a full, if somewhat bitter, life he found it hard to believe that he was shaken. As a newspaper man—one of the old type he was proud to call himself—he had seen violence in myriad forms and lived with it as with a chronic disease. He could not understand why a knot of fear settled in the back of his head or why he suddenly cursed himself for not having fireproof filing cabinets. All the unfinished work . . . all the unfinished work . . . and the big city papers trying to gobble him up. He looked about in despair. There were too many papers, too many documents to try to save. If the wind came with the fire, it would all be gone—all of a life, all of an era, of Sand Creek.

III

As the new City Planner of Sand Creek, John had no choice but to be at the office even though he knew there was little he could do. The fire department and the civil defense group acted autonomously. The police staff was too busy to speak to him. Everybody was too busy. An unusual silence hung in the darkened rooms of his department, draped over the electric typewriters, adding machines, and keypunch boards.

He walked between the rows of desks, trailing his hand over the machines as if over mountains. He picked up a phone, then replaced it before putting it to his ear. Harriet could take care of herself and shouldn't be waiting for a call from him. One was enough, even though that was some time ago. It would do her good to wait it out, even if the babies were frightened. Now that he had the job he wanted, they had to live up to it. His days of indecision were over—the days of fighting what his father wanted him to be. Now he could build, right from the ground. In Sand Creek he would have to; there were no foundations, no precedents. Each day was a concrete block. Harriet would do the decorating, the woman's thing. They would build the edifice of themselves.

Out in the hall someone ran by, the echoes snatched by the night-gobbling wind. Perhaps he could do something downstairs. The police were short-handed. At the bottom of the stairs he hesitated, looking down to the glassed office where the dispatcher sat. Mulvaney had just come in, his coat torn halfway down the back and blood dripping from his head.

"What happened?" he shouted down the stairs.

Mulvaney didn't look up. "Caught in a falling house in West Mesa. We just don't have enough men." He covered his face with his hands.

"What can I do?" His words bounced down the marble steps.

"Nothing, kid. You stay here. Or try to get home. You have a family don't you?"

"Is it that serious?"

"Yes, it's that serious."

Harriet and the children flashed across his mind again.

"I think I'll stick around," he said. He wouldn't be scared home, not by an old cop who resented him. They were the breed who just couldn't get used to the new city administrators and planners—his

10

father's breed, curse them—all afraid of something they couldn't understand, and all very unwilling to try to understand it. When he moved West, he had hoped to get away from them—the old men with their tenacious hold on the way things were, the men trying to keep things that way. But here were old men, too, worse than in Boston, for they had seen far less. Their views were bounded by the mountains and the plains. They despised city planners as much as his father did, or even more. They considered him a personal, rather than sociological, threat. And he was their first, here in Sand Creek. A kid they called him. A kid. He held their futures on his drawing board and they called him a kid. He could make their city grow—be beautiful—and they called him a kid.

As he returned to his office he thought of Harriet lying on the bed. The shutters and back door would still be banging. She would be awake by now, alert to every sound, guarding the house by sheer nerve, holding it together by strength of concentration.

At his desk he picked up the phone and dialed home. A loud buzzing stung his ears and he slammed down the receiver. She would have to be all right. He wasn't going to let it be said that he left his work when he was needed.

There was more than he could begin to handle—before this storm. They had given him an office, some equipment, and some vague directions. Then they had slipped away, resentful. He was meant to be a seer, to discover the lives—past, present, and future— of this ungainly city lapping at the mountains. In the process he had to discover the nature of every relationship—of official to official, agency to agency, and institution to institution. It was a maze that would take years.

In desperation he had begun with the new subdivisions to the east, the area with the most immediate needs and the least complexity of background. The core of the city would have to wait. His very office building was filled with mysteries beyond him. The greatest of these was Benj Southard, the Mayor—his boss—sitting now directly below him in that huge cluttered room.

He had come here because of Benj—drawn by a good salary and something more he couldn't understand, something almost morbid about the man himself, the enormous man and the threat of tumult about him. Even now he felt compelled to go down to see him.

The plans for the Applewood sewer system suddenly looked dead, bloodless in the semi-darkness where they lay collapsed over the drawing boards.

11

IV

The temperature, Harriet knew, was dropping. Margot's hands grew cold in hers as they sat in the middle of the child's bed with its new hard mattress that the child seemed only to hover over as she slept. She should do something about the gaping window. All the time more glass was flowing into the room and soon the frame would be empty. If enough wind got inside, she vaguely thought, it would push the roof up. She had read that long ago in a story about a hurricane. There was nothing to use. Sheets or bedspreads wouldn't be strong enough. Cardboard, perhaps. There were those boxes up in the attic left over from their move. She could pull them apart—but the enormity of the job made her close her eyes.

A slow rumbling entered the wind in the living room. The books on John's desk, maybe on the bookcases as well, were toppling over in an avalanche. Everything in the room would go unless she did something to stop it. Even old Betsy was finally awake, padding about in the kitchen. Harriet hoped, in a surge near prayer, that she wouldn't begin to howl in the terrible way of old deaf dogs. They had meant to put her down. When the baby came along they couldn't.

Right now she must assure the dog. That meant crossing the open room and going into the fire-brightened kitchen, leaving the children on the other side of the house. It would be easier once they were all in one place. She buttoned the raincoat, which she was surprised to find she still had on, and searched for the boots she had kicked off somewhere hear the bed. Margot looked at her anxiously.

As she opened the bedroom door a rush of damp smoky air pushed at her, almost forcing her back. Strangely it was full of the woods and brought memories, like a sudden room of familiar faces. It was pine and pinon and sage and grass, hot dry days and cold nights made of cloud, lichen rocks and mariposalily meadow. It was making love in an alpine marsh. It was alabaster mornings when the snowy mountains, cut quartz, sliced the blue sky apart until it hurt.

She pushed through into the kitchen and pulled the dog, too heavy to carry, back to the bedroom. Margot hardly seemed to notice the animal as she fixed her eyes on her mother.

"Is it a blustery day?" the child asked. The day, she meant, that Winnie-the-Pooh was borne upon the wind and Piglet became a balloon.

"A little like that," Harriet answered, remembering that Owl's tree had blown down. "It will be over soon."

The old dog, unable to climb on the bed, settled down underneath, pushing against Harriet's boots. She would get cold soon, as they all would. It couldn't be much past midnight, and the temperature would continue to drop all through the night until, by dawn, it was well below freezing, and probably snowing.

That was what the wind was all about. Higher up it blew all the time, regardless of the season. The jet stream, an airy tidal wave, rolled over their blue world unnoticed, while, like fish, they lived below in stillness. But now the elements had hurled them out into a strangeness.

V

The wind poured through the deep channel of the high canyon like a flood, pulling with it what it could east towards the plains. As they fell, giant fir trees ripped soil from the cliffs. Tangles of roots, exposed forest ganglia, hung from crevices. Small rocks, triggering miniature avalanches, crashed down to the creek bed, and the walls of the river-cut weathered years in the night.

Small things held quivering to the depths of their holes; there was no hunting for the food of the dark. The speckled hawk stretched his wings down tight. The buck pressed his mate against the rock wall. Down in the black water bridged with ice the trout pushed against the earth side of the stream, stirring with winter slowness as vibrations came and went.

The shaggy ponies and burros turned out on the MacInness ranch near the mountain road clustered head-over-neck-over-head in the three-sided shed. The elk which usually came down to share their hay stayed away; no bugling rode upon the wind. No cars passed on the mountain highway; the long-haired animals were alone. They moved, as one many-legged beast, when branches and rocks blew against them from the open side. Then, in no particular gust, the old shed collapsed upon their backs like a rider slumping forward. The many-legged beast started to run with its strange burden of the storm.

At the mouth of the canyon the storm stopped long enough to hurl three summer cabins onto the road. In one of these crouched Dick Emory, a sculptor, who had no real business anywhere nor any place to call his own. The state police found him soon after, superficially cut. They quickly got him to the hospital, where the waiting room outside the emergency room was already filled to capacity. At any other time they would have taken him to police headquarters and searched him for drugs. They would have held him in the county jail, where the sheriff made a profit by cutting back on prisoner's food.

Harvey Price, another man fond of sculpture, stood in his darkened living room listening to the wind tear his outside collection apart. In his new stained-wood house not far from the Coxes' he had never before feared for his belongings. The latest piece, structured out of aluminum like a child's jungle gym, had just gone up last week in the garden. Its creator, a young wisp of a man from New York, had flown out with it to assemble it himself, intricate piece by intricate piece. There was no insurance on it yet.

The world of local artists, too, was blowing up before his eyes, and there was nothing that Harvey Price could do.

Someday, a hundred miles away, someone—perhaps a child—might pick up a shiny stick with a hook at either end and wonder what it was.

And undoubtedly tomorrow, or next week, an atmospheric scientist a thousand miles to the east would pull a cup of wind out of the sky and sift through the dust of Rocky Mountain soil and granite. Somewhere along the way the scent of pine and of snow would have fallen. Nothing in that cup would be alive as the residue rattled from one side to another and dribbled its way into classification vials.

Loren Weiss was an atmospheric scientist already at work on the strange upheaval of the wind. At the government weather and tracking station high up the mountain above Harebell Canyon he watched the needles on the wind gauges spin out of control. Several of the other dials in the clinical control room lay dead, their life machinery outside smashed against the rocks and ground up into the essence of the storm. The light produced by the generator flickered and the red glow from the fire below on the mesa threw patterns through the room, highlighting different parts of machinery—buttons, lids, levers, lables. Down the hall in the specimen room a crash reverberated. A bottle of snakes or tundra mice had fallen to the floor, but that was not his concern.

He would never be able to get an accurate reading of the storm now. The bits of data he had might as well blow away, too. Henry Eldon, his superior, couldn't do any better in spite of the arrogance his slightly-greater experience generated. The next weeks would be filled with multiple-copy requests to higher echelons for more machinery, lunch hours filled with the filing of the different colored copies. And all the while winter would be closing in around them. The jeep would spin crazily on the unfenced turns.

Eldon would always intimate, without any direct comment of blame, that the results of the storm were somehow Loren's fault. He would see that his underling didn't progress because of the enormity of his failing and the massive expense of his mechanical losses. There would be no recourse. The machine of the Civil Service could never be made to understand. The officials in Washington would never be aware of the sound of this night's wrenching wind.

Under Loren's window of mocking light and shadow a snowshoe hare crouched against the wall. With one ear bent and bleeding and hind leg stretched stiff, it would struggle no more through the elements that had turned upon it. As it congealed with shock and fear, the firelight slipped over its marble coat.

Shouts from the firefighters echoed through the large empty house where a shaggy band had broken in. Like a cell exploding, the vandals scattered through the rooms. Then, finding nothing, they reunited and left. The sounds of the firefighters continued to slither through the house, up the stairs and down, into and out of closets, bumping against wicker furniture and sets of croquet and badminton. Glossed family pictures, taken many summers before, cast patterns of light on the floors.

At the hospital a young intern sighed as he sewed up the face of a child hit by flying glass as she watched the storm through a window. Some times it all seemed such an endless patching, such a random stabbing into gossamer, while the thing called life throbbed along underneath in its own mysterious way. Sometimes you wanted to shout at them, shock them, tell them you were only human, too, and that you didn't understand the components of their flesh, the mutual flesh. What medicine said was a placebo. Life was a mystery, making its own way, coming and going unaided, whatever he might do it its surface. He didn't understand.

Harriet tried once more to use the phone but found it still dead. Until the wind died there could be no contact with anyone. The house was cold. Almost all the furniture in the living room had been knocked over and papers blew everywhere. A large branch stuck through the shattered window. A few brown leaves were still on it, rattling. The curtains were over the couch. They wouldn't be strong enough—nothing in the house would be strong enough—to stop up the gap.

There had always been a strong house before, no matter what had gone on within it. She had never stopped to think of the crumbling process of a house, only of the crumbling of the people inside a house. To her, houses had always been endless vaults of experience. They were able, without outlet, to absorb one family chronicle after another.

In the farmhouse in Massachusetts that stood beneath the patient elms there seemed little to indicate the passing of time. The hollyhocks and tobacco grew. The grass came and the snow fell. Inside, the furniture continued unchanged from the eighteenth century.

After college it became a dream, a picture in a childhood book long put aside but remembered, warmly, in pieces. Scenes returned in three-dimensional slide form. In these she might have been one of Peter Pan's mermaids seen through a view-finder.

That her parents were dead now and the house gone could never alter it. Somewhere the house went on; anytime she could walk back in unannounced. They would look up and smile and talk to her of gentle things that never changed, pets and school friends and her garden plot where she made pretense every Sunday amid stalks of the previous summer's annuals. It went on and on. They would never let her grow older; she would never let them change.

Because they had died together mysteriously after she had moved West, she had never had to face the reality of a deterioration in them. They were safe. Without always realizing it, she talked to them, using them as sounding boards for almost every decision. John must never know. He considered her lucky to be parentless and tried hard himself to be so. Building up something new was enough for him. She wished it could be for her.

Up on the mesa a tangle of trucks, hoses, and men cast a confused pantomime against the backdrop of flames. From below it looked as if the work was going on in the wrong place, far from the main burst of fire further up the mountain to the northwest. It wasn't possible, from below, to see the big gully separating the men from the flames. There in the crevasse shovels dug furiously in the spotlighted dark. Occasionally, with gusts, the flames leaped out over the gully and made a roof of fire. If it got over to the other side and could not be checked there on the lip, it would flow like lava down the hill into the town, over the rooftops and on out into the empty plains. I could work its way down around the gully, too, by the north slope of the rounded mountain, or even down the south side. According to the direction of the wind it would advance, and the wind blew madly, as if from every direction at once. Dust in miniature tornadoes spiraled among the equipment. Burning branches sailed the currents like canoes.

Dicks, the Sand Creek fire chief, rested against the lead engine listening to the radio from headquarters. He knew he would hear there was no more equipment and that the fires out east on the plains were worse. The men there would have to cope as best they could. Now he had to decide how much equipment to send up around the gully to the north slope where the weather station was. There was a lot of valuable equipment up there, something to do with the weather satellite program, which the federal government would hate to lose, but sending men up there would mean letting the south slope go. The fire could work its way down into the town more easily that way. His men couldn't get him accurate wind readings. It was anyone's guess as to how long the blowing would keep up before the rain or snow fell. It would be another day, at least, before the Indian firefighters could get here from the Dakotas. He would have to decide. There was nothing to base a decision on. There had never been anything like it before, and he had seen plenty. He would have to go on a hunch.

Calls were coming in now from outside the county. Other places were beginning to get worried about the wind and didn't want to send much equipment out of reach. No planes or helicopters could fly. Lines were down all along the front range; they had no way of knowing what was happening in the high mountains. There might be a hundred little towns down the crest of the range burning up and there wasn't anybody to send to them. It might be burning like a river all the way down into New Mexico, or like an ocean over the plains.

The temperature began to drop and the dryness went out of the air. The smell of wet earth from the firebreak rose and mixed with the smell of smoke.

Dicks felt himself falling down through layers of experience. At the very bottom was life and death, beginning and end, things pushing against each other in the earth—seasons and worms and seeds and colors. The urgency of the struggle jarred him awake and forced him back up to the surface.

A new tub light went on, momentarily shocking the gully workers into motionlessness. A call came in that one of their men had been blown off a truck.

Out on the plains by the airport Dicks' assistant looked toward the glowing mountain. It was getting no better up there; they wouldn't be able to send men down to him. Soon he would have to let the hangars go; it was getting too dangerous for his men. Explosions were already ripping up the small planes on the west edge of the runway as if a hidden army were shelling them.

A metal roof coasted by like a seabird. Parts of a small plane, appendages of a ruptured insect, followed. All landed inaudibly in the open where the truck lights swept. Water, foam, and clods of earth tumbled through the revolving wind. Often the men were forced back. Soon they would have to start worrying about the power plant, the ineffectual but explosive tangle standing harsh against the sky.

VIII

As John entered the Mayor's office a swarm of men rushed by him down the steps. Benj was alone, slumped behind his desk. He couldn't be dead; someone would have stayed behind. But there was always an air of death around Benj, the huge tumid mound that seemed constantly about to crack. John felt himself uncontrollably drawn to the possibility of an explosion in Benj—of mirth, wrath, or whatever might lie beneath the straining surface. He felt he only had to wait long enough to witness it—the heaving of thick innards.

"Hello, John," the Mayor rumbled as he lifted his head. "What's up?"

"That's what I would like to know. There must be something I

18

can do." He hated to offer himself like a sacrifice in the ritual of waiting.

The Mayor rumbled inaudibly. Then, as vibrations took form, he softly said, "Can't say, my boy. You might try goin' over to the CD office and stirrin' up those old women over there."

John knew he was excused. Thankful for the errand he turned quickly to the door. As if attempting to catch up with the swarm he raced down the steps. He wanted, suddenly, to be in a group, not alone. He wanted, most of all, to be away from Benj. The compelling desire to see him was now a force of repulsion. He was glad to go out, anywhere. He sought clean air, even if it came in ripping gusts.

Why did he humiliate himself this way, serving as flunky to so unpleasant a man? It was almost as if he had sought out the most repugnant person he could find. Maybe his father was right; maybe he really didn't have the guts to stay where he was born and try to live up to what was expected of him.

When he decided to give up architecture and move west the whole idea had seemed so challenging. Perhaps there never had been challenge in it, only escape.

Harriet had not wanted to come. She said she could not imagine living anywhere but in New England. Now she had borne her children here. They were surely creatures of the wind and openness, nor did Harriet seem to mind, now that it was done. She questioned very little but accepted what was set before her. Like a field fallow in the autumn or the spring she waited for what the day would bring. Even her features seemed indefinite. With the distraction of the wind it was hard to see her face, shadowed beneath the wheat-like hair. He could not hold her in front of him, not with the storm tearing at him.

Had he married her because he sensed her to be so malleable, so unwilling—or unable—to offer resistance? What else could it have been for? Certainly not beauty, brains, or birth. She had very little, yet he had chosen her and taken her away with him to build a life he considered to be entirely suitable to him. And she had always done just as he wished. They had no problems, no sensitive areas. They were very lucky. All around him he saw marriages disintegrating, or people lonely, people wanting. There was Ren, their only friend here from back east, who had no wife, who only had his work.

On the street wires and trees blew wildly. What traffic signals remained hung precariously.

19

Neither of the two Civil Defense officers looked up as John entered. They had long since shut out all noise and the worry of what that noise could bring. Like a single person they raised their eyes when he greeted them. No, they had nothing to report. He might as well go home. Simultaneously they looked down at their desks again.

Outside the blank traffic signals continued to swing free, almost over the wires suspending them across the street, Several uprooted fir trees blew like tumbleweek down the empty avenue. Debris scurried for shelter.

He might as well go home. Harriet would be glad to see him, though she wouldn't admit it, appearing to have everything well under control. Perhaps Margot, if she were awake, would be glad to see him. It would be better than wandering around the municipal buildings, anyway.

Once in the car on the dark erratic streets he threaded through fallen trees. At Broadway and 17th, he hit a dog that jumped crazily into the road. He stopped to help it, though there was nothing he could do for it as it died dazed and uncomprehending.

There was no place for animals to go. Even people, away from their homes, were vulnerable. Never before had he felt exposed, not even when he shed his antecedents to head for the western mountains. That had been a game of spite; he saw it for the first time. Now he was afraid and shocked to find that his heart was beating rapidly. The wind rose up before him like a wall, and he knew he could not get over it.

IX

The neighboring houses were dark shut boxes. No one had come from them to offer help. But why should anyone? She had not gone to them to offer help. Indeed, except for some of their names, she didn't know them or anything about them. She had given them nothing. In all these months she had not even tried.

Now, with both the children awake, she could not go. Everyone outside might as well be dead. It might be some kind of an attack happening all over the country, or the world. It might herald the darkening of the sun or a huge power blackout like the one in 1965, just before her parents disappeared forever. How could any one

20

person, against such a huge force, be sure?

The wind became momentarily still. There was something happening in it, one of those quiet secret things of the sky.

The separate sounds of the ravaged living room became audible: the scuttling of paper across the floor, the flapping of the almost-severed curtain. Through the broken window came sounds of the mountain: half a shout, a siren, skidding tires. From the backyard there was nothing, nor from the bed itself where they clung. The chests of the children barely rose and fell. Even the dog abandoned the snoring of old age to lie silent.

A loud rattling knock shuddered the front door. John. She clumsily set down the children and ran throuh the adjoining room to the front hall and the door. A wad of papers pushed against the back of her legs as if trying to hold her. But he wouldn't knock, no matter what, not with the extra key outside which he had often used. It must be someone else.

It was a large man in a drab slicker who held a flashlight to her face blinding her.

"Husband home?"

"No."

It was no one she knew.

"We need every man we can get up the street to start ditching. Can't hold it on the hill much longer."

He was gone, already halfway to the next house. There must be some simpler, more efficient way of getting help. But, of course, without phones, even lights, there was not. Nothing was the same as it had been only a few hours before. Nothing was the same, nor ever would be.

The trees, still quiet, leaned down the hill. Their backs were broken, or they had given up resistance. The smell of the fire—of hot sage and juniper—was stronger; or did she only imagine it? Where was John, and when would he get back? She shut the door heavily and sat down in the ringing darkness where the papers flowed idly, in no particular direction.

If they were ditching right up the road, maybe it was serious, far more serious than she had imagined. She should start getting ready to leave. But where would she go? How could she just leave everything behind—all these things they had worked so hard to collect? John wouldn't have it. And he would be home soon. She would just have to wait.

As she sat by the front door she became aware of another sound on the porch: a walking, touching noise, a stroking. That man wouldn't have come back. He was the collector of other men; he had a job. What could someone else want?

With eyes adjusted to the dark, she picked over the rubble in the room. Things from the outside still slithered in through the window, half in, half out. Maybe the noise was only one of those slithering things—a vine or tree half dead with winter and the storm, half inside, half out.

Quickly she slipped the bolt, the second lock over the door. Slowly she pulled back the curtain over the window next to it. At first she could see nothing but the woodpile now messily toppled from its neat stacks. Then she saw it, rhythmically moving on the steps—a man kneeling on the walk, patting the top step with a slow, circular motion. He seemed completely absorbed in what he was doing. She watched him, as if in a trance, while he repeated the motion over and over. He stopped. She dropped the curtain and backed off running, to Margot's room. The children were where she had left them. The old dog looked up. Nothing in the room was changed but the beating of her heart, which now knocked against the walls.

She had to forget the porch. There was no one to whom she could go. It could just be old Denkle from down the street; he was always getting drunk, harmlessly, and ending up on other people's porches when he couldn't find his own. Or it could be some other harmless drunk more lost than usual because of the darkness. The darkness had drawn John away; it had drawn all the men away and left the women locked in houses. In the dark the houses were all alike. A drunk would never find his door.

The wind swelled. It rose and fell with the breathing of the children. She lay down next to them, trying to cover them in their confusion of angle. Her heart rocked them all with a rhythm which was even, though fast. It became a comfort in the dark.

Long ago, in thunderstorms, her mother had come to her as she lay in her small iron bed below the eaves. Her mother had always been able to recognize the climax of the storm.

"There, now," she would say, "that's that," and every time the crashes would diminish, as if frightened away into the distance to try someone else. What a wonderful quality it now seemed—to be able to recognize the climax.

There was the time father's machine business failed. Instead of prolonging a sense of disappointment, mother simply adjusted to the new circumstances and went on. That summer the first of mother's piano students came, waiting their turn on the swinging bench on the front porch by the hollyhocks. Their terrible, cacophonous sounds on the old piano soon became part of the house, another thickness like the leaves of the chestnuts and maples dark with the summer and sweet. She tried to concentrate on those leaves, veined like miniature maps.

The quiet, stable days of the house in Massachusetts afforded constant opportunity for examining detail. There were no brothers and sisters, no family confusions, no problems except the quiet ones of money, and they only meant that she seldom went away. The shapes of summer shade, the pattern of Queen Anne's Lace—she could pull it all back in front of her, whenever she wanted, like a magic camera. John would never understand.

The sudden rattling underneath Margot's window was not memory, nor the wind. Harriet jumped up, the children falling together in a heap and waking with a simultaneous cry. He had found his way off the porch around the house to the room where they lay. Minutes, or hours, might have passed. The sky was still black, starlight gone, nothing in its place. The childrens' crying rose above everything else, even the crashing sway of her heart. Surely the crying would rouse him, attract him, bring him in. She couldn't hush them any more. She wanted only to join them, to cry with them into a dissolved state—something no one would bother with, or even see.

She couldn't sing. She couldn't talk. The children were cold and frightened. The candles were all gone, and the flashlight which Margot clutched flickered erratically. Soon it, too, would be dead, and they would have no light. If he got around to the south, to the broken window, he would climb right in. She could do nothing to stop him. There was no one to stop him.

"Come on, Margot," she whispered, scooping up the children in the quilt and blanket on the bed.

"Where're we going?"

"Out to find Daddy."

It suddenly seemed very logical.

Lumps of bed clothes, they straggled to the door, then bounded to the garage and the waiting safe old Packard. With the children surprised into silence, Harriet sped the car out of the garage onto the street and down the hill—east, to the plains.

X

Up in the mountains, beyond the fire, a cold wind rushed into the vacuum of silence. Flakes of snow rode it like lancers. With huge scoops it scoured the canyon walls. Pine needles blew upward with the granite dust and hovered.

The living things of the mountains cowered. From their holes they watched brightly but with no motion.

The needles which were held aloft on the updraft began to thicken with snow. A heaviness pressed down upon the wind and softened the scouring. Snow dropped down upon the bare rock peaks above timberline, then upon the scraggly trees below. It slipped down further into the thickness of the forests. It filtered down to their lower branches and to their dark matted feet locked together on the floor. Single flakes clung to the lichen rocks. Lower still, snow sifted through the tangled branches of the cottonwoods looped over the streambanks. It settled on the ice, the roof of many trout.

Up in Harebell Canyon the firefighters looked up from the ditches.

"Snow!" they shouted to themselves and went on with their work.

Out on the plains, where the change in weather had not yet come, the wind still blew hot and hard. A bathtub appeared mysteriously by the side of the airport where the assistant fire chief still directed his men. In an hour enough boards had flown overhead to build a house. Most of the airplanes were gone, either burned or torn apart, or both. And still the wind-gorged fire scavenged, tasting ever eastward to the grasslands.

When he realized the dog was finally dead, John got back in his car. He had been able to do nothing but watch it; nor had the dog, totally wrapped in its agony, been aware of him.

Heavy, suddenly, with exhaustion, he started again on the tortuous route through fallen trees and wires. Now there was something new—snow—pushing against his windshield. It had bent the wipers grotesquely out of use. If it got much thicker, he would have to stop and wipe it off by hand. He shivered, calculating that home was still along way off.

At the corner of Thirteenth Street flaming boards fell across his path. It was no use. He couldn't get home now, not until everything stopped and it was light. Harriet would be upset, but he couldn't help that. He could do more here, where obviously every pair of hands was necessary. The whole block was in danger. There was no fire equipment in sight. At least he could warn some of those up at the other end of the street. It would be at least two hours until dawn.

Like one submerged he pushed against the car door. He must be getting weaker. The back of his head tingled and he shook the handle with rage. He had never been afraid before. He had never been held back, like this, from doing something that he wanted to. With a tremendous heave he pushed against the door just as the wind subsided. He fell, face down, in a tangle of branches on the curb.

There was no one to watch him; he could lie there quietly and wait. The smells of gutter moss, matted leaves, and fresh-severed wood came to him. He joined their tangle, something else hurled down and done away with by the wind.

He was, after all, useless. What energy he had, flowed in wrong directions. He could not help himself, nor Harriet, nor their children. He saw them sparkling down a parallel but divergent river, bending further from his sight. Soon they would be gone. He called out—an inarticulate shout of anger, fear, and warning—to stop them.

"What's that there?" came in answer, as a huge mackintoshed fireman bent over him, scooped him up, and set him on his feet.

Now, at last, he could get on with it and help save people from the block of burning houses.

At the foot of Canyon, Harriet was forced to a stop. Debris had turned the intersection into an obstacle course, even though no other cars were in sight. Turning north, up to John's office, was clearly impossible. She could go only straight ahead—to the east—or south. Either detour would be extensive. Now snow was beginning to slap hard against the windshield. The heater had not yet started to work, and they would all become very cold before it did. The baby cried in his blanket. Margot was silent, absorbed in piecing together what she saw out her window.

Bursts of flame grew like flowers in the dark. Fistfuls of wet snow exploded against the car, while bare branches whipped at it. The cloud of smoke, weighted by the snow, clung to the earth. They were choking in the closed car. Opening the window was worse—a mistake.

It was all a mistake. She should never have come out at all. But now it was too late to go back and deal with what was at the house. He might be inside by now, crawling in that awful way through the living room. Betsy. Old Betsy. She had forgotten her and had left her, deaf and all alone. She would have to keep going. If she could just keep the car on the road, eventually she would have to find some clear stretch. No matter where it led, it would lead somewhere. Once she got there, she could think things out.

But there was nobody. In all the breakage there was nobody.

As the car moved east the air lightened. Wind dispersed the smoke and kept the snow aloft, swirling between the earth and sky. She was getting out of it and leaving it, leaving it.

On the eastmost boundary of Sand Creek, on the edge of the plains which stretched on and on like a vision, there was a sudden freshness. She stopped the car on a rise to look back. There was only a trail of smoke behind her. The pink glow of the mountain fire rode over everything but it, too, was an aura, indistinct. There were no rocks, no buildings, no houses, no people. Even in the fields by the car there were no cattle, no horses, no sound of stomping and chewing and breathing. There was only the wind, still full of burning ponderosa, still too strong to stand in.

The baby woke up with a wail. The baby. The little girl. She had brought no bottles, no food, no money. Nothing. She couldn't just keep going. She had meant to look for John, to bring him back to help. Somehow she had forgotten. She had been drawn out here on the plains by something she couldn't remember or didn't know. She couldn't tell how long she had been traveling or what place she had reached. She opened the door and stepped outside to see.

The wind ripped tears from her eyes and blurred her vision. There was a line of fire she could see, just to the north of where she was—a long low line like metallic ribbon—nothing else.

A sudden thrust of wind threw her back against the front of the car. As she hit it she heard a scream that wasn't hers: Margot screaming as pain crashed through her own body. Margot. Where was she?

Bending against the protection of the car, she half crawled to the front door held open by the wind and looked in, calling. Margot was not there, nor in the back, nor anywhere by the car. The wind had died, leaving no noise. The air was still, sharp with the smell of burning pine.

She must find help. There was no help. The road was empty. She had passed no cars in all the time she had been gone. No cars in town, nor here. She was alone. They were all alone. Her parents, even if alive, couldn't help her. She must not blame them, nor John. He, too, was somewhere alone.

The child couldn't have gotten far. She had to remember that, keep herself, hold herself from running, wildly, into the night. She searched, first, by the car, going twice around it, looking under it, while calling all the time. The baby shrieked, held her back. But Margot. Margot. Come back. She made circles further from the car while screaming into the darkness. She crossed the road, stumbled into the ditch. The ditch. Children were always falling into ditches, falling and drowning. But this, in winter, was dry. Margot. Margot. Come back. Then she fell over her, Margot in the ditch. Margot in the ditch. Let her be all right. She picked her up and ran zig-zagging to the car. There the baby cried as if for all of them. Margot in the ditch, all quiet in a lump.

Harriet put the child on the front seat beside her and spun the car back on to the road. Without thinking of an alternative she continued east. There had been no help behind her, and Sand Creek was too far, too full of smoke.

At least there was, before her, the dawn—a thin sliver of light along the horizon. Already light in the East. People in New York,

Massachusetts already up and going to work. Busy. Normal. All jostling each other in the rush—parents and children and friends and strangers

Margot was absolutely still while the baby cried, convulsively, in the back. It was necessary not to think, just to get help. She must not look at her, touch her. The spell could be dangerous.

Fields and fields passed by and the tall tangled cottonwoods marking the streambeds. Telephone poles and wires and lean-to sheds passed while dawn spread up into the sky like a stain and Margot lay still on the seat.

Then it was there, a house up against the dawn, a real house—solid, white, with a porch and trees, even a garage and a barn.

Harriet skidded into the driveway and jolted to a stop. With one more look at the child, still quiet beside her, she jumped out of the car and ran up the steps to the front porch. A swinging bench and comfortable chairs. Curtained windows and a foot-scraper by the door. Everything, finally, as it should be.

She pounded on the door. Only then did she realize she was gasping, her heart swinging loose through her entire body. Outside of herself there was silence. She pounded again and called. There didn't seem to be enough air in all the outdoors to fill her lungs. Then the rolling of her heart began to seep out—through the porch, through the silent house. There was no one. It was empty. They were gone.

PART II

I

John left the group of charred buildings, happy that everyone was out, safe. Finally it was dawn and he could see his car. He would get in it and drive home, no matter what he met on the way. He would help nobody. The snow had lessened like the wind and the trip was quick, almost as if there were no unusual circumstances.

But Harriet, he realized when he saw the open garage, was gone. Why? She wouldn't want to leave a secure house in a storm like that. Old Betsy was howling lugubriously as he opened the front door. In the first dimness he could see nothing. Maybe she had just loaned the car to someone. Then an arm of papers wrapped around his legs. The window at the end of the room, he could then see, was blown in and everything toppled. There was nothing right-side-up in the whole room. She would not be in her bed, nor the children in theirs.

He picked up the phone. Still dead, of course, and no way to reach anyone—to start calling her friends to find where she had gone. Her friends: Frannie, down the road with her traveling husband who was never there? Lydia Whitmore downtown who preyed on the young for whatever energy kept her going? Or Ren Hadley, their friend from home with the three daughters? Hadn't she been going there a lot? Wouldn't she be there right now? He'd go right over. And be upset.

A tree lay across the Hadley's walk but otherwise an air of calm veiled the long low house built into the hillside. No one was about, and many minutes seemed to pass before footsteps came to answer his knocks. Only then did he realize that her car wasn't there—that he had only to search for her car.

"Hello, John." Ren Hadley, crumpled with sleep, could not help an involuntary start of surprise. He retied the belt of his bathrobe.

29

"Sorry to get you up, Ren. I thought Harriet might have come over, but I guess she didn't."

"Why should Harriet come over? No. Sorry, John. Is something wrong? Is there something I can do?"

There was nothing. Ren was very much the gentleman, and of course he would ask. No wonder Harriet liked him, with his very proper ways. She never mentioned him, but of course she liked him. Ren was a home a great deal, though his daughters were too old to need him. He should have thought about it long ago—all that Ren could offer, the very essence of gentility which he himself denied. It was something, apparently, important to Harriet after all.

Harriet's car was not at Lydia's nor Frannie's nor a number of other places he tried. She couldn't have gone far with the babies but he did not know where else to look. He was very tired. There was no point in wandering around when she was, undoubtedly, all right. He went back to the house to wait and was soon asleep across the bed.

At one in the afternoon, soon after most of the service was restored in Sand Creek, the telephone rang. It was the hospital, reporting that Mrs. Thayer and children had been admitted. Condition unknown.

The sun, around to the west, flooded through the open window facing the mountains. The last of the snow was melting in large clumps. Brightness whirled through the room, a kaleidoscope of memory. As he went out the door, old Betsy howled, once more forgotten and unfed.

II

At the hospital cots lined the two wings of the second floor. Over 50 patients had been admitted during the night and early morning. Many more waited on benches outside the emergency room in the basement. This information was imparted to John by a harried pink-uniformed volunteer at the front desk who wore three bands for her years of service. She had no idea where his family was, or who had called him. They were having trouble keeping track of admissions properly. A large stain ran down the front of her starched smock. Perhaps, she said, he had best start in the west wing upstairs and work his way east.

Harriet lay, unconscious, in one of the piles of white bunched along the smooth dark corridors. He recognized the lank straw hair.

"Shock," the intern said. No regular doctor was available, nor did anyone in Harriet's vicinity know what had become of the children.

John stood, where he was directed, by the nurses' station in the center of the corridor. Information was promised from a variety of sources. Telephones rang and uniformed personnel came and went around him. Metal chart boards were piled up and unpiled, trays of medicine brought and taken away. No one looked at him. Half an hour passed.

Finally he bent so far over the counter the sedentary head nurse was forced to look up at him. "Any information on Mrs. Thayer?"

"Thayer?" She flipped through a collection of charts as if she had forgotten him completely. "Dr. Randall saw her, administered a sedative."

"And the children?"

"Nothing here about children."

"But there has to be. They were with her. I'm sure."

I'm sorry, Mr. Thayer."

With one backward glance at Harriet, her face to the wall, John walked to the other end of the corridor, through the waiting room to the elevator. Men, women, and some small children—a heap of exhaustion—spilled out of the room into the foyer. He said "excuse me" to a young woman who leaned against the frame of the elevator. She held a paper bag filled with what must have been children's clothes; a small pink sweater was half over one edge.

John found his children downstairs in the pediatrics ward in a special room where they were being kept until identification could be made. Somehow in the confusion of their coming in—they were brought by a farmer who lived way east on Highway 3, the nurse said—they became separated from their mother. There was no way of determining who they were. Only emergency treatment could be administered until operative procedures could be approved by a parent.

"Operative procedures?" The baby was on his side, cooing and grasping at the bars of his crib, but Margot, he could see, was asleep.

"Yes, the doctor is waiting now." The nurse beckoned toward a man in white bent over a bed in a room diagonally across the hall. "I'll tell him you're here."

When she was gone the small room seemed very empty. The baby paid no attention to him but went on with his project of grasping and ungrasping the bars of the crib. Margot was motionless. He did not go to look at her. Next to her a metal cabinet with partially open drawers displayed an ominous assortment of equipment. There was nothing else in the room. There was no sound except for the gurgling of the baby. Through the open doorway he watched what seemed like frantic, though pantomime, activity. A long time passed.

"Mt. Thayer?"

The doctor was surprisingly young and obviously exhausted. He didn't wait for a reply.

"I've been very anxious about your daughter—in a real bind here. I need to operate. Very quickly."

"Operate? But she's just . . . ." Suddenly there were no words, no meaning. The bare white walls went awry.

"She's suffered a severe blow on the head and has been unconscious since brought in at seven this morning. I've done all I could. I need to operate immediately. All the papers are here."

He pointed to the top of the cabinet-table by Margot's bed. For the first time John noticed the bottle suspended over the child's head and the tube leading, somewhere, into her.

Mechanically he signed the papers where the doctor indicated. It was probably the first time, he thought with bitterness, he had paid no attention to the fine print.

Quickly a nurse transferred the child to a stretcher bed and rolled her away. The baby fell over on his back and began to cry. He waved his arms and legs furiously, like an overturned insect. John picked him up and put him over his shoulder, as he had seen Harriet do a hundred hundred times. Soon he was quiet. As the sounds from the hall came back, the enormity of it struck him. Margot was dying, his child, his own. And she had been dying, alone, in this strange white place all day, her blood leaking out somewhere in fatal patches. He had been asleep, alone. The baby became heavy. Without a word he handed him to the first nurse who passed by and stood by himself in the busy corridor.

At the end of the corridor there was another waiting room, identical to the one upstairs except for the prints—cities upstairs, clowns with balloons downstairs. He picked torn magazines up from the one empty chair and sat down. Around him bodies shifted in seats, legs crossed and uncrossed. Then all the room fell silent with one breathing. The monotone of the intercom, the rattling of trays, the swish of the elevator swirled around the organism of waiting.

The clock read two-thirty, of a dateless day.

The magazines were old and almost all for women. The artificial plants and the chrome lamps glared, pinning him in a painful cross-reflection.

He could not get up. There was nowhere else to go. He had to be near, though he could not bring himself to imagine the details of it. He knew nothing of it. It seemed impossible that he could be the husband and father, the one they had been seeking, the one around whom all the questions and the pain flowed.

Surely that young doctor was not the baby doctor. Who was he? What did he know? How had they gotten here? How could anything be so complicated?

Only yesterday—or was it the day before?—everything had been so ordinary. He had come home, eaten dinner, read some reports, made love with Harriet—or had that been the night before?—and gone into a dreamless sleep. Now Harriet was here unconscious. Margot was here unconscious, her skull being opened up—that tiny skull capped with hair as golden and mercurial as her being.

And Harriet. What was in her skull, that bowl of bone? He could not picture her. She was a person not of face but of hands, hands that were everywhere—shaping, warming, making. She was a kinetic force—a weaver, not a being complete in herself. The threads of time went through her hands and came out in children, meals, solid things. But she had no face. She had no words. She was the needle through them all, bright and soundless.

Maybe he really had married her because she was so indistinct. At the time she had seemed comfortable, workable like earth or clay. He sensed he would not have to struggle with her the way he had had to struggle with those around him. He wanted peace, and a slow building up of something that was his own. He wanted escape from those terrible summers when, home from college, he had to confront his father.

The long, low house on the dunes of the Cape was open everywhere to light but he remembered it in darkness.

It was winter now. Snow had come and melted. Sunlight had filled the wide-ripped window as he left. Something terrible had happened. He tried to focus on that window.

His first esthetic, or professional, fight with his father came over windows. His father, a classicist, was in favor of large formal windows.

John, eager to grasp anything new, considered paned windows barbaric, if not prissy. Ever since that argument (His father had called him a hopeless dilettante.), he had designed almost exclusively in slab-like effects to avoid conventional windows. Then he had given up architecture altogether. Suddenly it seemed not to matter. Maybe he was growing old.

He was very tired.

There had been so much fighting, about everything: where he would go to school, his marks, his plans, and then Harriet. No wonder his mother had given up and taken the ultimate escape into death.

When the struggle over Harriet began there had been only Ren Hadley—courtly Ren—to defend her. He happened to be back East on a visit when they announced their engagement. Ren, a former student and a long-time friend of John's father, had been able to calm him somewhat.

Now John tried to forget that. He wanted indebtedness even less than acrimony. How incredible they had all ended up in Sand Creek, caught between the plains and the mountains. Or was it? Perhaps he had been drawn to the town more by the knowledge that Ren was there than the lure of the job and the chance to move away from Boston. Maybe he came in a futile attempt to exorcise the debt. He knew now Ren would haunt him always, a prod to the memories he could not put to sleep. For this he tried to hate him but could not. Even now he thought of calling. Who else, really, was there? In a year they had found very few friends, and none with whom they could feel utterly at home.

The clock moved while all else stayed the same. At three, dizzy from watching it, he got up. Again there was a unified but wordless stirring of the room. He broke away from it and did not look back. Many eyes followed him down the hall.

He attached himself to the nurses' station where someone would have to come to him, speak to him. A hum made up of all the hospital noises surrounded him, absorbed him. He was at its heart. He was the hum, but no one came to him; they flowed around him.

A covered stretcher passed by bearing death or unconsciousness. He did not want to know which. Once, getting on a train to travel west, he had watched a coffin being rolled, naked, toward the baggage car. He and that coffin had ridden, together, through the night of the sleeping countryside to the edge of the winter plains. He had felt the weight, several cars back, being pulled by the locomotive. He had

34

tried, unsuccessfully, to climb out of his own weight and hover above it in that dimension of souls.

Now, again, he was part of a conveyance of life and death. Awful, awful, awful, he though in rhythm with the hum.

"I want to know about Margot Thayer," he said in what seemed like a very loud voice. He paused with embarrassment.

Without consulting papers the nurse answered, "She hasn't come out of the operating room yet.,,

"How long will it be?"

"I haven't any idea. Are you her father?"

It was a ridiculous and a sad question. There wasn't anything he could do even though he was her father. He had no idea what was being done to her, somewhere inside, by people he didn't know. He might never see her again. There was no way of knowing. He would go now to that other part to visit Harriet, to try to make some sense out of it. He began to weave uncertainly down the corridors.

Harriet stirred, turned toward him, opened her eyes fully and then shut them again. He could not rouse her. A nurse came, and she would not come out of a sedative for several hours, and that Dr. Randall would be by soon.

John told her he could wait only a short while and sat down heavily on the floor at the foot of Harriet's bed, his face in his hands. No, he told the surprised nurse, he did not want to wait in the waiting room. He had waited too long.

A hand was on his shoulder. "Mr. Thayer?"

The Dr. Randall, upon whom so much seemed to rest, had finally come. But Dr. Randall was disappointing: short, gnome-like, staring through huge thick glasses. How had their lives so suddenly come into the control of such unexpected people, he wondered? It hardly mattered; he was no longer responsible.

"Your wife was incoherent when brought in. We couldn't piece anything together. There doesn't seem to be anything wrong with her, but I wanted to talk to you before she came out of the sedative. I gave her a fairly strong one."

The doctor waited, as if for a confession.

"I don't know myself. But there's a child, our daughter, being operated on now, somewhere." He moved his hand n a vague, slow semicircle.

"Which doctor?"

"I don't know."

Abruptly Dr. Randall turned to the nurses' station and picked up a phone.

"It's not over yet," the doctor said, "But I think you might as well go ahead and tell her about it. I see no reason for keeping her here, especially with things as they are." He raised an arm toward the corridor and was gone.

Two men died that hour in a room not far from Harriet's bed: Jake Cole, the fireman who was blown off his truck during the storm, and Joseph Netter, the Pine Street recluse whose roof had collapsed on him as he slept. Dick Eddy had been found dead in the wreckage of his car off Highway 7.

Upstairs a fourteen-year-old girl gave birth to the twisted baby she had failed to abort.

The quiet of a November twilight dropped upon Sand Creek. The leaves scratched along the earth until a cloud, heavy with cold moisture, pressed down from the mountains. The lights sank into an aura and noise became indistinct.

"I've done what I could for her," the young doctor was saying again. "Drained and relieved pressure where I could. But we just can't say yet."

"Thank you." What could he say to these strangers who had suddenly become the arbiters of all that surrounded him?

When he returned upstairs, Harriet was ready for him.

"You never meant to come home, did you?"

"Of course I did.'

"But you couldn't have. You killed her."

"She's not dead."

"Where is she then?"

It was useless and he walked away. He collected the baby for whom he had no clean clothes, left the hospital and drove home. While still in the garage he heard the dog howling. No one, he carefully calculated, had fed or walked her in twenty-four hours.

The coldness of the house shocked him. He pushed up the thermostat even before he flipped on the lights. As if walking into a lake, he became colder with each step deeper into the house. The debris, finally, made him stop, and he turned back, into the bedrooms.

The beds were torn apart. Harriet, he suddenly realized, had never before gone out of the house without making them; she felt their tidiness to be as important as that of her clothes. Appearance was more important to her than anything, though she was so hard to picture.

First he would have to take care of the dog. Then the baby. What did he eat? Harriet, he remembered, had started giving him bottles. He could have some canned formula. After the dog. Then he would have to get diapers. Clean the place up, fix the window. That first, before more cold came in. The papers around him continued a life of their own.

The baby, after a remarkably long period of silence, began to squirm and wiggle. There was no place to put him. The crib. The dog crying. The papers on the floor dragging at him like hands. He couldn't make it all come together, not possibly.

Before he realized what he was doing, he had heaved himself in the telephone chair and dialed Ren Hadley's number. He didn't even know he knew it and was almost surprised when Ren himself answered.

He had hardly moved from his chair when Ren arrived with two of his three daughters. While they hovered for a second on the threshold in the halflight, they appeared as tall, handsome, and supple as gods. Then they were gone, scattered through the house to their unassigned tasks. Everything would be all right.

Nan, the youngest—and also the blondest and most beautiful— immediately scooped up Jeffrey and had him silent. Ellen, the second daughter, went in the other direction to old Betsy in the kitchen. Like summer aspens they stirred vibrations. Before John could gaze after either of them, however, Ren led him to the window, the gaping wound that must come first.

"What supplies do you have in your garage?"

"Not much, I—"

"Your plywood worktable. It will do for now. Come on, we'll bring it in."

Ren, of course, was right. The slab of plywood was just what they needed. There were even hammers and nails, almost anything a carpenter could want, lying on top of it. The four of them were able to hoist it up and hammer it in, stopping the flow of night. With a fire in the fireplace and the furniture back in place, the room began to appear normal. The girls even managed to get the curtains back up, though one was badly torn by the branch they had to disentangle from it. There was no more communion with the dark.

"I'll have some food for everybody in a jiffy," Ellen said on her way back to the kitchen. "Harriet certainly had everything in good order."

"Harriet." Ren said, in the first possible moment of confrontation, which John realized he was unable to avoid. "How is she, John?"

"She's all right. I think she'll be fine. It's Margot. I should call now."

"It's hard to tell about children so young. They can survive incredible things."

Alison Hadley had died of a cerebral hemorrhage just a year before on Thanksgiving night.

Ellen came from the kitchen with two strong scotches.

Nan came from the bedroom with Jeffrey, whom she had changed and dressed.

"It's a lucky thing," she said, "that I was over last week to sit for them so that I know where everything is. There's plenty of everything, just as if she'd known. I would never be so prepared."

"Prepared, my love?"

"No damage at your place?" John asked.

"Only a couple of garbage cans and some small trees outside," Ren answered, "and a lot of soot blown around inside."

"And the terrace door, Daddy," Nan added.

"Oh yes, the west terrace door was ripped right out of its lock. I guess that happened quite a bit. I doubt there are many places in Sand Creek tonight tight as they were night before last."

As the three Hadleys began to talk simultaneously, the aura of godliness about them dispersed. The spell of concentrated intensity— THE EFFORT TO HELP—was broken, and they were people again, friends and neighbors.

The four sat, with the dog and the baby in their midst, in a close circle on the thick rug in front of the fireplace. When Ellen broke away to return to the kitchen, the others drew together, sealing the gap. The baby touched each one, laughing.

"Think of all the looters tonight," Ellen said merrily as she came back with more drinks and a plate of sandwiches. "Tuna fish on the right, bacon on the left."

"Looters!" her father snapped. "All you young people seem to know is looting and revolution and arson. You're hardly a friendly generation. Why should people want to be out looting? I'm sure there are many more people out helping than there are out robbing. How ghoulish!"

"Oh, Daddy!" Ellen counter-exclaimed. "You're so romantic!" romantic!"

And he was, John realized with a jolt of recognition. Everything about Ren—from his physique to his pursuits—added to a mystique of romance. Even the events of his life, like pieces of a mosaic, built up the picture of Camelot. There seemed little about him that was random. Death itself bounced off him as off a shield, leaving him younger and more idealistic yet. He seemed to expand, daily, with the conviction that Alison was happy, that they were all working to build something together.

With his impossibly beautiful daughters surrounding him, Ren could stake his kingdom anywhere, even here in Sand Creek. Suddenly it was clear to John: Ren really was out to build a fortress, one quite capable of flying flags from turrets on the first of May or swinging drawbridges up and down.

"Your cultural complex, or conglomerate, or whatever you call it—how is it coming, Ren?"

"Ah! The great hope. It's good to think about while these kids' looters are out and around. I don't know, John. The Mayor. He's so concerned about the money. He just can't seem to see beyond the budget in front of his nose. He's definitely not sympathetic, and I'm sure he'll try to sway the City Council. It's not a question of money, you know. We can arrange for that easily enough through federal programs. I don't know what makes him so opposed."

"He's not what you'd call a man of culture. I don't know what he is. It's as if there is a darkness over him. I keep trying to figure him out but get nowhere."

"He's strange, all right, Benj is. I sometimes think he visualizes himself as a feudal lord here—can't stand the thought of any interference. You're one, you know, though he had to hire you. A planner might do away with him. He's an anachronism, and he knows it."

"The whole city's getting to know that. I think he's getting desperate."

"I suppose that's why he resents all us outsiders so much. But when he asked me to start that group—the Committee on the Role of the Arts and Letters—I thought he was sincere, not just trying to get me off his back. Ally said CORAL was a joke, some kind of lure to keep me from what was really important. She said—"

Ellen leaned across him to collect the sandwich plate.

"She said," Ren continued, "it would be an empty building. A beautiful but empty building because it would have no rooted spirit of its own."

"No, Ren, it doesn't have to be. What with the university here growing as fast as it is, there will be an increasing need for such a place. The community will want to keep up with the university, and, indeed, to pull ahead of it. Pride is very important. It'll work."

"I really don't know. Sometimes I think it's insane. I should go back to Cambridge, at least somewhere where they'd understand."

"Oh, I think they understand all right. It's a question of whether or not they're ready for it yet."

"Here we are talking about 'they' as if 'they' were a bunch of idiots. They're not. They're people, like us, who give their lives, or a good part of them, to the place where they live. They want it to reflect them and grow with them. It has to be spontaneous, coming from them. Why do we—I—push for something they don't seem to be ready for? We really are outsiders, you know, though we try hard not to seem so."

"That's just you, Daddy," Ellen said as she returned. "You couldn't *not* push."

"No, I suppose not. I think it's important—establishing a criterion for taste and providing a milieu for its expression. It seems, somehow, my special job here."

They were all quiet. Still, no one heard the door open or felt the cold air slide towards them. Harriet stood watching them for some time before they were aware she was with them.

"Harriet!" Ren cried. With his back to the door, he was the first to feel her.

"Hello, Ren. Hello, girls."

As if confronting a spectre they got to their feet and slowly went towards her. Crumbs and glasses marked the boundaries of the abandoned circle.

"I know you didn't expect me, but there was no point in staying. There's no room for any more. And Margot's not . . . ."

Her voice trailed off, but John could not help her. Even Ren, for his perfection, was at a loss. They had all discovered each other in a horrible secret. There was no need to pretend otherwise and make it worse.

"The baby's all right. He's sleeping," Nan ventured.

"Let me get you a sandwich," Ellen suggested.

"Thank you. Thank all of you."

"Yes. Thank you. All three of you," John added, finally able to talk. "I can't . . . ."

"It's all right," Ren said. "It's what we're here for. Call us anytime. *Any* time, Harriet. Do you understand?" He shook her slightly by the shoulders. Then, as gracefully as they entered, the three Hadleys left.

IV

The sound of the door closing bounced against the boarded window and knocked around the room.

"I didn't think you would just leave me there, not knowing."
Harriet spoke rapidly. "There was so much to do—trying to find out, trying to find the children, the doctor. How could you just go off like that and leave me not knowing?" She broke into crying and flung herself across a chair.

"You weren't fully conscious yet and you weren't being reasonable. I couldn't stand it there any longer—all that unconsciousness. I had to get out. I'm sorry, Harriet."

He had to be patient, gentle—lie to her—even if she wouldn't listen. Something terrible had happened that he would never fathom.

Carefully he picked her up and took her to the bedroom. She felt oddly boney, like a large bird. He shuddered as he put her on the cold bed. She held herself stiff, even when he stretched her out and stroked her back and legs.

Harriet seldom cried, at least in front of him. She tried hard to hold her features in place, ephemeral though they seemed.

He could not call her out of the paralysis. With an involuntary sigh he got up from the bed, covered her with a blanket, and walked out of the room. He pulled down the leash from the front hall hook. Bending down in front of old Betsy, he suddenly threw his arms

41

around her thick shoulders and put his face in her tangled, matted chest. The dog swayed uncertainly. He steadied her and led her out the door.

Outside the fog had lifted, replaced by a sharp cold. A storm of stars spread overhead, surging up from behind the front range. Each peak, like obsidian, cut blackly into the sky.

In the lower elevations, not yet purified, the smell of sodden fire lay in pools.

In front yards debris filled the corners and spilled out onto sidewalks and gutters. Inconceivable things obstructed him as he led the blind dog meandering up the block toward Harebell Canyon: cushions, bicycle wheels, ladders, paint cans, a toilet seat. He met no one.

Rays of light from behind boarded windows bisected one another on the lawns.

He followed Canyon Street uphill past the more opulent and unconventional houses. At the top the road ended in a circle meticulously landscaped with sandstone and pinon. Beyond the last row of planted trees the mesa grass took off, wild and sweet even now. A hundred feet further up the hill gaped the last ditch, where the fire held. From there a black carpet of ash spread up to the base of the mountains.

Betsy balked at the ditch and would go no further.

It was good enough. From there he could look back over almost all the city, twinkling like a dim reflection of the Milky Way.

After the detached vignettes of the preceding night, it had come together: myriads of lights in swirls. There was no pattern, even in the subdivisions far to the east on which he spent so much time.

Harriet was down there and Margot—the one cataleptic, the other, perhaps, dead. He was at their center. He should be with them. He should be at his office. So much work would need to be redone—the study of the greenbelt purchases, the budgeting for emergency procedures. The drainage in the subdivisions would have to wait and his reports on the zoning requests. Benj would be furious.

He must think of Harriet. He forced his eyes down the quiet street to his roof. He forced his view below it. He must see her, really see her, stiff upon the bed.

He had left her there, under that roof—anchored, he thought—AND HAD GONE ON TO OTHER THINGS. Somehow she had been unable to hold up. Something had given way; he would have to discover it and build it up. If he were patient and very gentle, maybe he could discover what.

Betsy tugged at the leash, whining to go back. He let her pull him toward the road.

He was not that kind of person, but he would have to try. If her were to continue unhampered in his work, he would need to have her strong and utterly consistent. He had always taken comfort in her lack of resistance and what seemed a responsiveness to his needs. She had to be there for him, right behind him. Otherwise he would be back in the same morass of struggle; he would get nowhere. Everything his father warned would come true.

At the gate he kicked away some trash which had piled up in his absence. Strangely, there had been little wind while he was gone.

Inside, the acrid smell of smoke was very strong; he hadn't noticed it before. Within it, there was a silence. The baby, bunched against one side of his crib, was deep asleep, a foetal shape.

Harriet, too, had softened into sleep. He lay down beside her and drew her into the cove of his body. As he whispered in her ear, she slowly turned over on her back and opened. He pushed up her nightgown, the one he had watched her put on night after night, and kissed the smoothness of her stomach. She arched slightly and he put his hands beneath her. Perhaps none of it had happened and he would have her once again.

He could not pretend he did not need her.

In the morning she was gone. To the hospital, John figured. He was surprised to find that it was nine o'clock. The Mayor, as well as John's own staff, must have been waiting for an hour. In spite of his heaviness—the weight of body and of atmosphere which hung about him—Benj was punctual, and he expected everyone else to be.

John was less surprised to find what he did in the mirror as he shaved. A layer of darkness had settle into his skin. He tried to remember what day it was but gave it up. The work was there waiting for him, no matter what the date.

PART III

I

Ren Hadley marveled at the order of his life. The storm had hardly touched him, while it had brought destruction to all parts of the town. Boarded windows, town roofs, mangled antennae, charred houses, and piles of extraordinary debris had marked their route home from the Thayers'.

With the girls he again checked the house. Still nothing seemed out of order. As he settled into bed he expected something to occur—a huge noise or cataclysm. But everything remained quiet. He could almost make out the words of the late news downstairs. Order, perhaps, was the compensation for loneliness. He must, really, get a smaller bed. He could even use a smaller house. One child was already gone, as soon the others would be. He didn't need all this space. He couldn't fill it. Instead, it pressed upon him, made him smaller.

During nights, and windy nights especially, its interstices grew enormous, as deep and cold as areas between two stars. He was afraid to walk then and went to bed early, holding still on the side that always had been his, in stillness wearing out a trough too narrow for soft sleep.

Last night, the night of the storm, he had been more afraid than he could even fully admit to himself. Necessarily calm with the girls, he had felt himself ripping like the dry limbs of the winter trees and watched himself scattering, flakes of a small being over the flat high plains.

As usual he awoke without an alarm at six-thirty, slipped into his sweat suit, and quietly left the house to jog through the neighborhood up to the small park and back.

A line of pink pushed up against the horizon to the east. To the west night still lay across the mountains.

The houses in between were ordinary, really. Very ordinary. He wondered how he had come to be in their midst, for he was no ordinary person. There was nothing egotistical in thinking that. By birth and training he was no ordinary person. Yet here he was in the heart of so pedestrian a neighborhood, with his daughters growing up around him, one already grown and gone and totally beyond his sphere of influence. With Ally dead, why did he stay? There was nothing to keep him here, or anywhere. The job that brought him out here—of masterminding cultural exchange programs for the federal government—had long ago turned out to be a farce. Anybody could have handled it. They did not need a blueblood, though they tried to use him. Why didn't he go back, to Boston, where he felt comfortable and at home? Why did he stay out here, like a second-rate ambassador relegated to an unpopular post?

Perhaps it was the challenge of the lack of esthetic order. More likely, he had recently come to fear, it was an inability to face competition. On a frontier one expected less. He had only to perform competently to satisfy his eastern peers; they would not expect him to achieve great things.

But why did it persist—this fear of not living up to potential—shadowing him? He should have buried it with Ally, his last real bridge to the East, when she was scattered in the mountains, in a flurry of light .know, a year before. She had wanted the break to be complete, for him more than for herself. She did not need a break herself; she could have lived here, or there, or anywhere unshadowed, a person of full light, tall and strong as an obelisk. She knew his needs and acted quietly upon them. Nobody could have done more, but then she left him when he needed her the most, when his work collapsed and the girls were almost gone.

At the park Ren flopped down on one of the solitary benches between the playground and the Greek-style amphitheater. Squirrels scampered off and flickers flashed red to the trees. The slats of the bench creaked inhospitably and then all went quiet.

In spite of the mountain backdrop, always incredible, the park, too, was ordinary. Without the front range it would be ugly. Mentally he stripped away the granite—the awesome planes of tectonics piles up one on top of another. Left with only a slender line of elms and maples, all imported from a more gentle climate, he shuddered with a fathomless loneliness. The dry cold cut through the sweatsuit and tightened around his damp skin. He was getting too old to enjoy this sort of thing. Soon, what would there be left for him?

Mrs. McGovern, the housekeeper, greeted him cheerily as he returned. He was struck by her neatness. Her heavily piled hair never seemed to release so much as one strand. In half an hour she would have a breakfast of perfection ready for them all. By noon she would have cooked dinner and cleaned, polished, washed, ironed and run any number of errands. Even then, he suspected, not a wisp of hair would be out of place.

The wind had brought no damage either to Mrs. McGovern's house nor to her daughter's. They had much to be thankful for.

At his office the same remarkable sense of order prevailed. The mammoth fort-like building erected almost a decade ago for his use stood inviolable. More than wind would be necessary to mar its purposely rough facade. Inside, the rows and floors of offices radiated brightness and efficiency as always. Faces turned up, in respect, as he passed. The name plate on his door was newly shined. His desk was clear, the view from his floorlength window was serene. From eight stories up the town looked unchanged. The only difference from any other day was the absence of his secretary. When the phone rang, he answered it.

"Ren?" Harriet was surprised.

"I thought you'd still be asleep after—yesterday."

"No, I couldn't. Ren?"

"Yes, Harriet?"

"Could you come down here, Ren? I'm at the hospital."

"Of course."

"I'll meet you in the lobby. Right away."

"I'll be out this morning, Tracy," he called over his shoulder to his secretary hurrying across the parking lot as he got into his car. She would be surprised; he was himself. Suddenly remembering, he almost turned back to ask her if she experienced trouble with the storm; she had never been late before.

The way to the hospital was still unaccountably littered. He thought of Harriet driving there alone, veering around the same bunch of wires, the same tangle of fence and shutters. With John so preoccupied, and so insensitive, it seemed, she would have to cope with a great deal alone. She hardly seemed independent, though he scarcely knew her. She seemed afraid of him, undoubtedly because of the role he played as intercessor for her a number of years ago. How strange that was—that he had been there on the Cape—a chance visit—when their private storm broke. He had seen nothing wrong with the girl; why shouldn't he have supported her, especially since John really appeared to love her? Hang Wainright Thayer and his pugilism. Now both Harriet and John were lost as friends, and Wainright, too, though he mattered less.

Harriet was probably unaware of much of the role he played in her behalf, but John was very much aware of it. As a result, he would never let either Harriet nor himself get close to him. It was surprising John had moved to Sand Creek and not tried to stay as far away from him as possible. His reaction was entirely understandable, but sad. They all needed each other. As newcomers, displaced like himself, they needed him; he could do much to help them get established in the community. As an aging and still uprooted foreigner, he needed them, a link with what he had left behind. He did not like to estimate how much.

So much of his life consisted of mandatory official socializing he sometimes wondered if he had lost the power to discern what was real in people. Bureaucratic superficiality had begun to seep very deep inside him, and he let it; increasingly, he let it. He should get away from the job, away from everything that was an excuse. Now that the girls were old enough to be by themselves he could start again. He must really set his mind upon some kind of renewal. The Civic Center that now controlled so much of his energy was not a renewal; it was a last attempt to commit himself to the strange life he had chosen. He would fail.

II

Harriet, waiting for him inside the front door, sprang on him as he entered.

"Ren. Oh Ren, thank you for coming."

He pushed her, almost roughly, away from the front door to a corner behind a phone booth, the most secluded portion of the large marble room.

"Harriet." There was no gentler name for her. "Where's John?"

"He's—I don't know. I just came. I didn't wait."

"Is Margot . . .?"

"She's still unconscious. They might have to operate again. The doctor's been here with her since very early."

When will John be here?"

"I don't know. I didn't ask. Take me somewhere, Ren."

She had gone all into eyes, a lake. Her face, her mouth—every other feature—was drained and colorless. Even her fingers appeared transparent, like the fins of a fish. She had shrunk away from collars, sleeves, and cuffs. He almost put out his arms to pick her up, but she grabbed his hand and spun him around to the door and out to the parking lot, where she had already pinpointed the location of his car. She clung to the door until he unlocked it and she could get in; then she waited stiffly until he was beside her.

"Do you want to go home?"

"No. I want to go . . . somewhere . . . somewhere." She shouted the last words then threw her arms around him and sobbed.

"Harriet. Don't. Don't." He bent over her and shook her gently. What did one do? One distracted, shifted attention, offered something bright. It had been such a long time.

"Come, let's go get something to eat. I'm sure you haven't had any breakfast, or last night—"

"No." She looked up at him calmly, almost as if unaware of her outburst, unaware of the melting of her face—never very pretty to begin with—and of where they were—in the busy parking lot by the hospital entrance.

"No," she said again, less calmly, with a shudder. "I want to go back to the house where they found us. To thank them."

"Where is it?"

"It's east. Take Three. I think I'll know it. I don't know how far."

As if released she became tranquil and set about straightening her hair. Her fingers wandered hopelessly in the hay-colored strands, finding nothing.

"I bet you don't even have a Kleenex." He smiled and handed her a starched handkerchief.

She folded it into minute squares of thickness. "You must be busy. I shouldn't have bothered you."

"No, not really. As a matter of fact, not at all."

He hadn't been busy for seven years, not since he moved out here to take over the government program. It was remarkable, but true. He could take a week off, or a year, and it would make no difference. He hardly needed the salary. They hardly needed him.

"You know, Harriet, you mustn't blame John. He *is* busy. Very busy. He's starting fresh in a very new field. And with a hard man to work for. A monster. I don't know how he does it."

She looked into her lap. "I shouldn't have called you."

"Yes, you should have. I told you to—anytime. I meant it."

He put his right arm around her shoulder and pulled her toward him. Her head slumped against his side, and immediately she was asleep.

Absently he drove around the town. There seemed to be no place to take her—not his house, nor hers, no any other. He could not take her far from the hospital.

The driving was difficult. He would have preferred to stop, but she had to be kept warm, and asleep, for as long as was possible.

He drove carefully, filled with an overwhelming sense of fragility around him. Why had she chosen him? Did she really have no one else she could turn to? It was bewildering.

The central part of town—the old town—was chaotic with fallen trees. Many houses lay mangled beneath shattered elms and maples planted decades before by settlers. The Victorian Findlay house was broken almost beyond recognition. Ren gasped when he saw it, for he had always held a special love for it. Only recently he had convinced the Historial Society that they must buy it when it became available. It was to have been his special project, containing a library on local history that he was to build up through the years. Another attempt that would fail.

Down the hill, in the commercial section, the yellow caps of work crews bobbed everywhere.

In the south section where he, Harriet, Mrs. McGovern, and Mrs. McGovern's daughter lived, the damage was extraordinarily random, more like the work of a tornado than a general wind. One window would be smashed and the one next to it intact. One antenna would be severed, the neighboring one still straight. Certain houses, with torn-off roofs and collapsed walls, looked as if they had been singled out for destruction.

Ren found himself wondering about the occupants. Many were out, wandering about their places. He drove by his house to check it once more. It was as neat and as pleasing as ever, though the juniper definitely needed trimming. He sped up, hoping Mrs. McGovern had not been looking out a window, though it was unlikely. He stopped suddenly for a large branch across the road, and Harriet woke up, looking wildly around them.

"Ren! You didn't take me. We're not there. We're only— here."

"I didn't know where you meant, Harriet, and I didn't want to wake you. I wanted you to sleep, It's been about an hour now. You must be getting hungry. Shall we go somewhere?"

No. No. I hoped you would take me, that's all. I thought you would. I was very important. I better get back to the hospital now."

"What about the baby?"

"He's all right. I left him with his sitter. I better get back now."

Her plaid coat became enormous as she huddled against the door, staring into her lap. In the last hour she had shrunk even more. The squares made him dizzy; he couldn't look back at her but kept his eyes on the road. He put his right hand out to reach for her left. She didn't move and his hand fell against her thigh. He couldn't think of anything more to ask and fell silent beside her. The trip back through town was quicker. Already the clean-up crews had made a difference.

As he got out of the car she stiffened. He helped her out and led her through the parked cars up the ramp to the revolving glass doors. Inside he placed her on a couch where she resumed the same position as in the car. The couch was covered in black and white hound's-tooth, a pattern that ate away at Harriet's plaid and threatened to consume it.

Ren went to the information desk to find out what he could. While waiting for the pink-uniformed woman to make her calls, he went to the phone booth and looked up John's number. John was not in. No, there was no message but his name; no, he could not be reached.

"Are you the father?" the woman asked as he returned.

"No." He sighed with the realization that it would do no good to explain that he was a father, had daughters of his own, that he was ready to become the father of all daughters if need be. It did not seem to matter to her, anyway, for she did not try to withhold information.

"She's in intensive care, and the doctor will be ready to see you in a few minutes. That's upstairs, west wing, the end of the hall." She turned to someone else beside him.

Harriet held to the same position. He could not bear to look at her any longer. Convinced John would appear, he went out the front door to wander up and down the parking lot. Perhaps John simply didn't realize how serious it was for Harriet. Perhaps he hadn't really seen her and just didn't know. But John was the one who would have to get through to her, to find that terrible gash in her spirit and stop it up before she leaked entirely away. He was going to have to strengthen her with love. But how could he say that to John, a man fifteen years younger, a man so different in outlook? A man who, already, owned her? What if the child died? It seemed likely. Would John be strong enough for both of them? There was the baby, an infant. What would become of him? It was a strange and frightening burden, but he must, somehow, assume at least part of it and do what he could to help them.

An ambulance rolled into the entrance below where he stood. He sought, against his conscious wishes, to see who or what lay covered on the stretcher.

As he sought the face, John bounded up to him out of breath.

"I was just on my way up when you called, Ren. Got the message."

"You've got to do something for her, John. I don't know what. I can't get through to her."

"Let's see the doctor."

"He's waiting upstairs. But I don't think Harriet—"

"You stay with her down here. I'll go."

He gave Harriet a perfunctory kiss as he rushed by on his way to the elevator. Ren sat down with her.

"He was just on his way when I called. He's going to see the doctor now. You needn't worry about it."

She only drew further into the enormous squares of brown and purple.

"I'm going to get you something. Wait here." Confident she wouldn't move, he went in search of the coffee shop. Someone would have to fend for her, lead her; yet, she was not pitiful. He wanted to know why.

When he came to her support back in Massachusetts, he did not know her. He had met her only once at a large cocktail party given for him the night he arrived. Even today he hardly knew her better. But now, as well as then, he had the feeling that there was more to her—that she held a certain reservoir of interest.

At the party she made him think of a very delicate spring flower discovered in raging summer. She had more than a simplicity about her. She had a blush, a hint, a sense of possibility. On the strength of that possibility he had defended her against Wainright's desires for a more suitable, and presentable, daughter-in-law.

"Harriet. Harriet. I have something for you. Some tea, and a sandwich. I don't think you've had anything to eat for a very long time. Please take these. Please Harriet. For me."

Silently she took the cup and plate. She held them awkwardly on her lap, afraid to move either.

"Let me help you. I'll hold the cup while you eat."

Obediently she handed him the cup and began to eat the

sandwich. After a few bites she reached for the cup then handed it back. When she was finished she put the plate down and looked up at him for the first time.

"Harriet, you've got crumbs all over you."

She let him brush off her coat, solemnly waiting until he was done. He tried not to smile.

"Now when John comes down we're going to take you home and put you to bed. I'll send the girls over after school and they'll take care of everything. They'll pick up Jeff and do whatever needs to be done for him. Maybe one of them could spend the night, even for the rest of the week, and I'll send Dorothy McGovern over to help. She'd be delighted."

"You're very kind, Ren. Much too kind. But I can't say no. I can't seem to get pulled together."

"Don't worry about that now. I'm glad you can't say no."

John caught his eye as he came down the hall and shook his head.

Ren helped Harriet up and together they went to meet him.

"Still not very much news. I think we'd better go home. There's no point in staying here. I've got to go back to the office, darling. I know Ren will be happy to take you to the house, and I'll be there as soon as I can. The Mayor's about to pop. He thinks he's lost a city."

As they drove through the town, Harriet looked about, taking notice.

"It's been awful, hasn't it, Ren?" she asked twice, as if a sudden visitor. The clean-up crews had almost finished their work. The streets and sidewalks were clear.

The house was dark and still smelled of smoke. Soot lay in thick sheets. The girls hadn't time for any real cleaning. I might even be necessary to call in professionals, Ren thought as he looked at it. Together they stood in the front hall, still unbelieving.

"It's hard. A hard thing to come home to. But I want you to try to forget all this and go to bed. We'll take care of the house."

"It's so cold. How can I just go to bed?" She sank to the telephone chair near the door. "It's dead. I can't. It's dead."

"You have to. I'll take you." He scooped her up and carried her toward the bedroom. She was as light as a child.

"It's been a long time since I carried a girl to bed." He gently kissed the top of her hair and hugged her. Nan, he supposed, had been the last, but often the other two woke up in the night. He couldn't remember.

The sight of the open rumpled bed made him start. A sudden shock, like pain, went through him. He couldn't put her down on it. It was alive with energy. It would consume her.

Pulling at his arm, she let herself down. He heard the bed groan as he sank to its edge. Harriet pulled harder on his arm. His face came close to hers, and she threw both arms around his neck.

"Ren. Ren. Hold me, love me. Love me."

She was breathing hard on top of him, pressing him down. The smell of smoke and flesh came up around him, suffocating him.

"No, Harriet. I didn't mean this. It won't help."

She was remarkably strong, pushing him down again into the mustiness of the bed. He wondered if he really should struggle. She sucked against his mouth; he couldn't breathe. He could let himself be pushed down; he could sink, melt, become what she wanted. Once he pulled away something would break—a strand of possibility that bound them.

"No. Not now. It isn't the answer." He grabbed her, rolled her over and sat up. She came up with him and for a second they swayed together with lowered heads. Then she thrust herself away, sobbing. He covered her with the bulk of his body and let her cry. This time it had to come, even if it overwhelmed her. He wouldn't belittle her with words of comfort.

After she had fallen asleep, as rumpled as the bed, he went out to the phone to call his house. Nan had just gotten back from school. She would come right over and he could leave when she got there with the baby. He went to the living room and sat in front of the fireplace with its black, acrid pit. He traced the pattern of crumbs on the floor, over and over, until he heard a knock at the door.

III

His house was empty. He couldn't remember ever before being home at four in the afternoon. He wandered, displaced, from room to room. Nothing creaked, nothing moved. The antiquity of his books and furnishings—the reapings of his life—wrapped around him. He wondered if he hadn't become part of them, the natures of collector and collected fused. Perhaps he had ceased to exist and this was the afterlife he had fashioned for himself: eternal hours of walking through collections, collections neither good nor large enough to inspire. He did not deserve more.

The rows of jade, the shelves of tea utensils—the Oribe, the

53

Raku—the walls of sketches seemed to go on forever, though the house was hardly large. Some was inherited, some was bought, some by him, some by Ally. All of it was random. He wanted to destroy it but felt no motivating anger, only lassitude.

He made himself a drink but still could not sit down. If only there were someone, almost anyone to talk to. Even Mrs. McGovern would have been a comfort. There was John. Maybe he should call John and try, again to warn him, but what could he say? John had to feel it for himself, know what to do without directions from him, or he and Harriet were lost to each other. Why did he concern himself with them? Would his responsibility for them never end? He had his own responsibilities. His own.

The office would be worse than the house, the upstairs worse than the downstairs, the living room worse than the kitchen. He could not go outside. He did not have dog to walk, a child to lead. He functioned unnecessarily. He was a wanderer through buildings, buildings of unwarranted grandeur built by other men. And now he was giving himself to another building, a building that was full of selfishness, a building that was absurd, but one he could not yet abandon.

What did it mean, his sense of shrinking within the buildings he knew? Was he letting himself be swallowed up, after all? He needed to break away, to make a visit, to have an experience—to do something that would give him a sense of himself, not just a sense of pressures on himself.

He looked at his watch—4:15 in the afternoon. Thursday? Or was it Friday? He could catch an evening flight to New York and visit Joanna; he hadn't seen her since summer, after she graduated. The girls would be all right. Mrs. McGovern could be happy to come over, perhaps with her whole family. They would all do well without him for a few days. He could stay at the club, wouldn't have to pack much, or phone the office. Just some shirts, an extra suit into the small suitcase he kept in his bedroom closet. A bottle of scotch. Some socks. He'd pick something up for Joanna when he got there.

In twenty minutes it was done; he was on his way. The road across the plains to the airport was dark with an early night. He might be anywhere—a fugitive from anything headed any place. Almost every set of headlights was the same, and every set of tail-lights. It was an endless road of back-and-forth beneath a starless sky. He might have ceased to travel. There was no noise from outside, no rush of air, no sensation of speed. A Toronado, after all, was built to overcome external sensation. There was only the static-crossed voice of Glen Campbell within, "I'm a lineman for the county ...." The girls loved him, and his manufactured sadness. They would like to be here now, headed east for an adventure. He had lost their sense of fun—or perhaps had never had it. Responsibility and work had always come first. This trip was a responsibility—to himself and to his family. He didn't try to keep up with them and had let Joanna go almost completely. Soon she would be beyond reach, and then one by one the other two. He didn't try to keep up with them and had let Joanna go almost completely. Soon she would be beyond reach, and then one by one the other two. He didn't even know what she was doing, only her address, with a few vague comments on postcards.

From behind the airline counter a uniformed arm reached out for his credit card and soon returned it with a sheaf of narrow papers. Legs hung down from lines of seats and feet crashed over shining floors. He was on his way.

The plane settled into a dark sky between clouded stars and clouded man-made lights. Ren let himself sink into the softness of his escape, the three-hour hiatus between what lay behind and what lay ahead. So much had happened in the last two days. Was it really only two days? The storm could hardly have settled. Down below it must be blowing still, the last gusts falling down upon the Colorado plains, reaching towards Kansas, reaching towards Nebraska, reaching, perhaps, toward him in the plane, safe at thirty thousand feet. Or was it safe? At forty-six he was growing old and afraid. Visions of the dead had come to him that night—two nights ago—in the storm: his brother, lost over China, and Ally, as well as others which came indistinguishable like a fluttering of hands. He felt them outside the porthole now and pulled down the shade against the night.

There were maps, magazines: *Vogue* with a staring of huge eyes above a jeweled throat. Not Joanna surely. Though she aspired to gaunt looks, she had too much of the country about her. She was made for the Wessex hills, not for Manhattan. She would never make it as a model. He had told her so over and over. But, of course, she had gone to do it, and it really didn't matter what he said. Perhaps he didn't matter, either. She was a grown woman now, motherless and independent.

Somewhere an infant cried. The plane dipped slightly. He would not pull up the shade and stare into the dark, searching for Chicago, or Pittsburgh, or whatever foreign city lay below. It would be someone else's city, webbed with light and thought not his own. He lacked the strength to work his way into such a webbing. He floated, eyes closed, his inward view clenched upon the mountains deep in summer. The softness of deep green came up around him, and the sound of alpine streams, bubbling up against thick moss with small white flowers.

Perhaps any city would be foreign, even a young one, a country one.

In any city would come that web—of people spinning out their lives, of adding layer upon layer of complexity upon each other. Sand Creek, with all its seething of mixed motives, was no better. His own motives were confused enough. Perhaps he should move into the mountains or simply spend his time traveling. A base at one of the clubs, in New York or Boston, would be sufficient. He could not make a house again, a nest where there could be no nesting.

As the plane landed, Ren could still not pull up the shade. He knew what was there, did not yet feel ready for it. Only after the plane was empty of its weary-eager load, could he pull himself together. The last stewardess, her face let down, was beyond politeness. It was just after midnight, New York time, and 34° with a slight drizzle. Western newspapers lay crumpled on the seats.

God, let him be quiet, Ren thought as he got into the taxi, but the driver was too intent upon the freezing drizzle to prod him for intimacies. He could keep himself closed, at least until the morning. He thought of Harriet, her essence leaking, draining into a void of fear. How vulnerable they all were to a hemorrhaging of spirit. There were autistic children who feared a touch would kill them. There were the hemophiliacs, but much could now be done to stanch their flow. There was all the rest of humanity, supposedly normal, so sensitive to touch. He tried to imagine pain—the pain of burns and cuts—but could not.

The night clerk at the Oak Club tried with obvious effort to disguise his surprise and displeasure at being aroused so late. The-last-gentleman-in-the-house-was-in-by-10 look was dark across his lined face. To satisfy him, Ren apologized to him then kicked himself for doing it. Egalitarianism could be carried too far, damn it. Why didn't the man apologize to him—for the weather, for anything?

In his room Ren opened the suitcase and took out the scotch.

Holding it, warm, in the only bathroom glass, he pivoted slowly. "Welcome, Renford W. Hadley, to Manhattan, city of your yearning, city of your past exploits, city that holds you captive."

The bottom of the window shade rattled as the wet night made a sudden stab.

The only love he ever knew was bound up in the wet-night sounds and colors of Manhattan. Even now she floated up to him upon the wet-night scent: a bright blonde girl of twenty, too beautiful, too gay to be overshadowed by the war, too beautiful to be dimmed by anything. Right now, he knew, she floated there above the street, her hair stretched out upon the lights like a swimmer's in a shallow pool.

As he went to the shade to lift it, a scream of obscenities shot up; it could have been male or female. He closed the window without looking and threw himself, still dressed, upon the bed.

IV

Late that same night in Sand Creek, Harriet decided she could never again sleep with John, or in their bed. Covering herself with a blanket on the couch, she determined to watch television until there was no more to watch. John, she could sense, was too preoccupied to notice, or to care. When he did, in the next couple of days, she would make some excuse. There really wasn't anyone to care about what she did, or didn't do. She was free.   She must accept her freedom and stop trying so hard to be dutiful. Dutiful to whom? For what? Even the way she had decorated the living room was a process of being dutiful. Why didn't she let anything clash, or a picture hang upside-down, or not at all?

Now it was mangled, but she would not try to fix it. Not now, at least.

What should she do—pray? She hadn't done that since she was very young. She wouldn't know where to begin.

She had nothing to do except run the machines, keep them all going, call repairmen when they failed. To how many repairmen had she opened the door and offered superficial talk? To how many people had she talked? To John? Never. She had simply gone away with him to be his wife.

During the midnight news (Vietnam casualties . . .) Harriet jumped from the couch, snatched her coat from the closet and ran out the door, not closing it behind her. The news followed her out: "A University study concludes there is no evidence that UFO's come from outer space . . . should drop further investigations . . . the Air Force . . . ." A weakening stream of light dissolved at her heels. She had disappeared.

John wouldn't follow her. She wouldn't let him. She wouldn't be called back, caressed, made to feel like a child. She would be a child only when she wanted to, when she slipped into the mechanism of the magic camera, when it was all right to be a child.

Nor would she let them chase her away. She wouldn't run. She would do her job.

The hospital entrance, at 12:20 a.m., was locked. Inside was a semi-darkness and no one visible. Walking around the building to the emergency entrance, she looked up at the windows, all in darkness or semi-darkness, as if a main switch had been thrown.

Once inside the emergency hallway, she was neither questioned nor observed. She held to one wall until she reached the stairs.

Outside Margot's room she stopped to look through the glass wall. The room was empty, except for the child under a jungle of tubes and wires. Glancing about her, Harriet slipped inside and up to the bed.

In the half-light the child glowed with whiteness. The whiteness was her only strength. Her breathing could make no rise in the sheet over her, could make no sound, could give no affirmation. Except for her whiteness she was invisible, inaccessible. The filigree of tubes caged her in a shadow-web.

Harriet could not unlock her arms to reach into the cage.

"Mrs. Thayer?" A gentle voice came up to her, slipping around her like an arm. "Such a lovely child. I've come to check her chart."

Miss Grimes stood beside her, looking down at the child. Thin gray and frail herself, the nurse had a definite face which Harriet knew she would never forget.

"Has there been any change?"

"I think not, Mrs. Thayer. The doctor was here about an hour ago."

Miss Grimes had beautiful eyes, eyes that spoke loud above her voice. Outward from them radiated the wrinkles of her face, like concentric circles from a splash. "I know. I know," they said.

Harriet moved closer to her. "Is there any—?"

"I don't know, Mrs. Thayer."

exuberant with beauty, a beauty of men's making, a beauty that could really be.

The apartment buildings with their doormen gave way to antique stores and drugstores. He crossed over several blocks and began zigzagging. He had no appointment this bright day in January. He wanted to miss nothing.

Outside a Schrafft's he stopped, then went in for breakfast. Always he had found it difficult to bypass a Schrafft's, with its combination of darkness and brightness and the taste of ice cream in metal dishes.

He sat at a narrow table with an old woman to one side of him and two young businessmen to the other. He wished he had thought to buy a newspaper or even to bring a book, as a shield. He would have read anything, to protect his meal. Then, when it was over? Had he some errand, some chore for somebody else? Harriet flashed across his mind. How many things she needed, and how little he could do for her. He couldn't give her health for her child nor strength for herself. He wouldn't demean her with a present, though he thought of Tiffany's, not too far away, and Cartier's. Perhaps at Jensen's, something more practical. No, there was nothing. She would have to wander in her own arena until she found an escape or turned it into something else. Maybe he should call John, or the hospital. He checked his watch. Almost an hour and half had passed since he called Joanna. On his way out he tried her number again, counting fifteen rings.

He would stroll towards her place, perhaps meet her there, or on the way. The sun had grown hotter, the streets more filled. He unbuttoned his overcoat, considered taking it off but decided that would be too awkward. Baby carriages came out alongside him, and dogs, and deliverymen. He felt caught up, less independent.

Suddenly he stopped, magnetized by a shop he remembered. It was a small linen shop totally unremarkable except for the fact that Ally had led him in there three years ago on their last joint trip to the city. She had seen a lace tablecloth, made in Portugal, which she felt she had to have. They had held it to the window and watched the light stream through the crescent moons and stars. She did not even ask the price but took it and used it frequently, even on that last Thanksgiving, when everyone had been together.

Joanna. He would find something for Joanna here. What would she want, a model? Not clothes and handkerchiefs and books and shoes and bags and candy. There were more tablecloths, and wedding veils, and towels. Place mats. Lovely, delicate place mats. She could use those, surely, no matter how she lived. He took a box of eight, with matching napkins, wrapped, and in a bright pink bag. At the corner he stopped at a phone booth. After four rings there was an answer.

"Joanna?"

"Yes?"

"Joanna, it's Dad."

"Daddy! Where are you?"

Yes, she would be in and he could come, but wouldn't it be better if she met him somewhere—somewhere for lunch in a couple of hours? She named a restaurant, a French name, close to where she lived and said she would meet him there in two hours—12:30 sharp.

Ren put down the receiver slowly, staring at the papers at his feet—newspapers, gum wrappers, shopping lists, a doctor's card, a shredded letter. She must have wanted to make it easier for him. He tapped on the machine. Curiously, a dime dropped into the return slot. He pulled it out, picked up the pink bag and continued on downtown

The crowds became heavier and his coat felt like a tremendous weight on him. The pink bag jolted against his leg. He switched it to the other hand and wiped the sweat from his palm. Two hours. He was very tired and would soon have to stop. Walking the sidewalks was different from walking the plains and the foothills. On the Tundra he could never catch his breath but enjoyed the feeling of suspension, the closeness to clouds and the dizziness of height. That weekend before Ally—they had watched a marmot chirping angrily at them from a pile of rocks, and clouds like enormous legless animals had passed over them in silence. They had gotten on their knees to see the frozen mass and wondered where the mass of alpine flowers had gone for the winter months. What a curiously prophetic conversation that now seemed, there on the outpost of the world.

At a small coffee shop he hesitated and then went in, buying a paper at the door before sliding into a booth. The *Pueblo* crew, the *Apollo* crew: the strange travels of mankind seemed to dominate the news, along with war and every kind of crime—the strange travels that kept them all in motion. His body had grown heavy. Had he really become old? Shouldn't he, as he had been advised so often, "get out and enjoy himself''? Maybe there wouldn't be much time. There was no way of telling, of course.

The table was dirty, the floor littered. Coffee would come in a thick glazed cup, almost too heavy to lift. How could he walk the next twenty blocks? He didn't have to talk, but there was too much time for anything else. Too much, too little time. Too much. Too little. A litany of the human experience, so quick to happen, so quick to end.

He read the entire paper, even the classified and personal advertisements. He folded it all up neatly and put it on the table in front of him. Spilled coffee moved like a brown cloud over the print until it was expended.

The clock over the cashier's booth read 11:20. He would call Harriet, then his sister-in-law, if he had the energy. At an inside booth he sorted out his package and coat, extracted his credit card, and made the call. There was no answer. He had no energy for Cara. She would not know, not care. Snatching his things, he headed for the street and Joanna's restaurant. *Le Petit Cachon Vert.* How absurd. Why not a good restaurant, a really good one, and then a bit of shopping—the way it had been before? Because it was not the way it had been before, you damn fool. He scuffed his shoe against a tree-guard.

Inside the restaurant it was not all bad; he would wait it out, anyway, with a drink or two. The few waiters seemed only too glad to leave him alone. He should have gone and gotten Joanna, but now it was too late. Or she could have come to him; but why should she? Joanna had always been grown-up beyond her years; he had felt somewhat in awe of her.

Eventually, along with struggling groups of lunchers, she came. At first he did not see her or know her. Her hair was pulled back tight against her head, with her enormous eyes heavily made-up. She wore no lipstick and a huge black cape, covering almost all of her. He got up, beckoned to her.

"Joanna," he called out loudly, surprised at the sound of his voice, "Joanna, it's you."

"Yes, Daddy. How are you? What a surprise. I had no idea."

"No, I just decided, all of a sudden, to come see you."

"To see me? Why?"

"Why? Because—there was a storm. I was tired. Oh, I just wanted to see you, sweetheart. I'm glad I could."

Joanna remained quizzical, guarded. Her eyes were bright,

strangely bright, ringed with shadow, not just mascara, shadow that dipped almost into the hollows of her cheeks.

"Do you find that odd, my dear?"

"No. Yes. Well, I mean, it is unexpected."

Her face was white, almost a glowing white, throbbing with her breath.

"How are you, my dear?"

"Me? All right Daddy. Let's not talk about me. What else are you going to be doing here? How long, and all of that?"

She was interviewing an alien, about to deny him visa, access. He had come with only good will, the best of will, and she would send him back, unknowing and embittered. It was a moment at the Hungarian border.

"I've come for you, Joanna. For several days. Two, now. I want to know about you."

"All of a sudden?"

"Not all of a sudden. Always. I haven't been able to get East for some time."

"Well, I'm all right. You needn't worry. Tell me about something. I never hear. I haven't gotten a letter in—not that I care. I'm all right. I'm doing fine. I have a good time."

She brushed the back of her hand across her forehead as if hot.

"I want to know something about what you do, Joanna."

"I work. I travel around. I visit. I go to parties. Mostly I have a good time. Let's forget it."

"No, I won't. I don't think you are all right. I don't think you're all right at all. I want you to come back with me."

"Back there? You must be joking. I'm all right, I tell you. Let's change the subject, or I'll leave. I've got some things to do. People are waiting for me."

"I'm sorry, Joanna. Sorry to interrupt your day. I thought—"

"It's not interrupting. It's just that everything is so different now."

"I fear so. I'm going to go back with you, Joanna, to your apartment while you pack some things. You can leave with me tomorrow, or we could go tonight."

"But I can't. You don't understand."

"I'm your father, Joanna. I do understand. I think you're not well. Your mother would have had you come back."

"Is that why you're here—because of mother? Do you think you have to be her?''

"No, of course not. Joanna, I don't understand, but I want you to come away with me.''

"No, Dad. I said no. I've got friends, commitments.''

"Who?''

"Moon, and Oatsie, and others.''

"Moon? And who?''

"Oatsie. Oatsie, and I'm Gypsy.''

"You're Joanna Hadley and you've been away from home too long, my love. Come, we'll go get your things.''

Ren motioned to the waiter and prepared to leave.

"You can't make me go, you know. I've things to do. Work.''

"Do you, really? I know you don't have to.''

"Sometimes. Yes. I've got things. Why did you come?''

"Why shouldn't I? I'm your father.''

"Still—now that I'm a grown-up girl?''

"Still. Always. I can't stop, you know.''

"Maybe you'll have to someday.'' Joanna looked as if she were about to cry.

"I don't think so. Are you ready?''

A sudden gust of wind hit them as they walked outside. Involuntarily Ren shut his eyes. When he opened them he saw Joanna staring into the wind, the stream of dust and leaves and papers. Then it died, falling at their feet. He pulled her down the sidewalk, towards the address burning in his head. She pulled back as if her cape made it impossible to walk—a toddler in too grown-up clothes. She was becoming heavier, more bulky. She was dragging further and further behind and he could not pull her anymore. He let go of her hand, and she stopped.

"Joanna, it's not much further. Please come along.''

"I can't, Daddy.''

A swarm of people passed her on either side, laughing.

"You have to, now come along.''

He didn't look back. They were almost there. The lower east twenty's. His daughter. Twenty-two? Twenty-three? A Vassar graduate. A Hadley. With these people, in this place. Ally. What would Ally have done? She always knew. There was never a fuss.

He found the number and leaned against the wall of the stairs. Joanna straggled up to him. There was nothing he could offer her. The pink package fell to the sidewalk. He had no plan, no program, no words except "come." He had no hold over her. He couldn't do it.

"Let's go up, now."

Without raising her eyes from the sidewalk she pulled her keys out of her pocket and handed them to him. They dangled from a miniature ivory skull worn smooth. He fiddled with them until he got the right one in the lock of the chipped and initialed outside door.

Inside there was no light. He let her move past him to lead him where they must go. He followed up two flights of stairs to a door in the middle of a dark passageway. She handed him the skull, letting him grope, again, for the correct key. As he found it, she put a hand on his arm, drawing him back.

"I'm home, now, Daddy. You can go."

She pushed past him into the room. He could not see past the black cape thrown up in front of him. The door was shutting.

"Joanna. Joanna."

His voice grew louder. He heard it dropping into the darkness in front of him.

"What's going on there?" came a voice from that darkness in answer.

"It's all right, Moon. You can go, now, Dad."

An enormous darkened figure came up behind Joanna.

"You can go, now, Dad. You heard the bitch."

The door closed, forcing him back.

He shouted and pushed against it but nothing happened. The door had gone smooth, a colossal, monolithic slab without handle or hinge or frame. There was nothing behind it, nothing to reach for. He left, running with terror to the light of the street. Once outside, he held onto the railing, gasping, a diver up from impossible depths. It must be age; he couldn't breathe. It came so quickly. He must get home, get home and save whatever there was left, stretch it out until he had done something, finished something.

The pink package was still there. He picked it up and held it in front of him, both arms wrapped around it. There would be a taxi one block over, or two. He would get back to the Oak, lie down, sleep. Later he would know what to do.

VI

At lunch time John drove to the hospital. He knew Harriet must be there. She wouldn't have just gone off, disappeared, not so long as there was Margot. And if there weren't? There was still the baby. There was still their home, all they had built up together. Physical surroundings—things—were so important to her, and he had done everything possible to make them what she wanted, to give her anchors, walls, to fence out the plains and the sweeping, haunting distance from where she had come. She had not come from much. She had seen very little; she was hardly ready for more, could not withstand large vistas, only what could be seen in miniature, only what was framed.

Rushing along the hospital corridor—he had to be back for a one o'clock meeting—John passed Harriet asleep again on the bench by the elevator. The coat flung over her caused no recognition. People seemed to be heaped everywhere. Never again would he be one of them, molded into resignation upon a waiting-room seat.

Margot was under two pairs of arms, two pairs of busy hands of nurses working. Only the slight rise of her feet was visible. There was nothing of her left. There was no point in staying, asking, wandering about, waiting, wondering, asking, asking, asking. When the time came they would come to him. They could find him, reach him. He would not go away. In the meantime he would go where he was needed.

A man from Washington was coming, an urban affairs officer, to talk about funding the new municipal building—Ren's strange dream. Benj would do everything he could to discourage the man and then would give Ren a different story. Ren should be there but wasn't, of course, invited. How odd it was, his devotion to this city that would never be his own, that could never be his own.

When John was growing up—at twelve, fourteen, or so—his father used to talk about Ren Hadley as the best student he ever had, a man of real promise but one too much of dream to do what had to be done. After Ren gave it all up—he walked out of his office at some big New York firm—his father was more reserved about him, spoke of him almost as of one dead. Then Ren had moved away and seldom come back.

Now he, too, had given it up and moved away and become as one dead. He hadn't spoken to his father or written to him in longer than he could remember. He had tried to keep from thinking of him but could not. His father lived inside his brain admonishing still. Their argument was not yet through. It was more than an argument, of course. It was a battle, a duel, which could not remain forever unresolved.

Benj belched as John entered his office. He swiveled around in his enormous chair from side to side, grazing his stomach against the side of his desk.

"It's about this s.o.b. from Washington, you know. I don't want any mollycoddling from you, you ought to know. Hadley's committee got this guy to come but I don't want any of him. We don't want any handouts from Washington, especially for something we don't need. We don't need it, John. Understand? We don't need it."

"I thought it'd be harmless. But it's not. That guy's gone crazy, all out of perspective over the thing."

"He's a competent person. If he has a job, he'll do it well."

"Too well. But you're just like him. You're the same—people from back there who come out here to tell us how to do things. You even talk the same. Wouldn't be a bit surprised if you two came out here together just to make trouble. I don't want it, and I don't need it. Hear?"

"I know you don't want it, Benj. I've been aware of that for a long time. But I'm not getting in the middle of this thing. I'll do my job and answer questions honestly. I'm not taking sides."

"It wouldn't be very healthy for you to get involved. Not even to answer questions that would help those people out. Understand?"

"I'm not so sure I do understand. Is that a threat? Does it really matter so much to you?"

"You can make up your own mind about those things, you know. I'm only telling you—and I run this town, you know—it wouldn't be healthy for you to get involved. We just don't need any more messing around in this town. Now you can leave, John. I'm appointing you my official representative to Fireman Cole's memorial service over at First Baptist. You don't have too long to get there, now, so you'd better be on your way. I want a full report. Understand? You be there, up front."

As had happened over and over before, John left with relief, not anger, glad to be released from the terrible presence. Only later would he feel the humiliation, the sickness, which would have to come. Then he would regret what he had done and search himself—just up to a point—as to why he had gone through it without screaming "Stop!" Surely there was a better way of life. Why couldn't he find it, or at least go after it? At thirty-one how many more years would he have?

For now it was enough to escape, to be a prisoner set free, at least temporarily. A Friday afternoon in January. Clear. Sharp. Winter energy burned everywhere like an electrical storm in complete blueness. To touch a tree would bring a shock; to smile would bring laughter, explosive laughter he could not control. He looked at his feet. The pavement sparkled back, alive. Strength flowed by him like a river. He wanted her, Harriet, away from what had happened, Harriet set high upon a mountain peak with shards of winter light pressing into them and cutting, throwing pain upon the snow.

Patterns spilled through the stained glass windows onto the pews and the floor. It seemed inordinately bright, John thought, for a funeral. The light, the mosaics of color, the electricity of the blue air washed over the coffin as if it were unimportant, or as if were a permanent fixture of the church. He could see only part of it. Evangeline Southard blocked his view.

Of course she would be there with selected wives of councilmen and minor dignitaries. She was far better a politician than Benj; if anyone could save his position for another term or so, it was she. Undoubtedly she had already instituted a fund for the family of the fireman. She had written to every member of the fireman's family. She might well have sat among the mourners at the funeral parlor, bowed in a vast silence that expanded towards every wall.

Evangeline, like her husband, carried a bulk greater than her physical shape. They might have been brother and sister instead of husband and wife so similar were the atmospheres in which they moved. "Look out for Evangeline. Look out for Evangeline," he heard echoing in his head. But then, he had chosen them—at least Benj—and had refused to extricate himself. He let himself be sent forth—an errand boy, an underling—by a man gone dead inside, a man breeding rottenness as he walked and talked, a man who wanted to destroy him, personally as well as professionally. He must break away from this morbid dance and do his work unhampered. Surely there were people, cities, where a planner would be welcome and appreciated. They could start over. They could get away from Ren, too, and that curious tie with the past. They could get away from his idealistic views of their role as gentlemen. Let it all be done. He would not be a gentleman.

Evangeline shifted to whisper into the ear of Kitty Conners, the zoning board chairman's wife. The mole on her cheek came to view. The coffin lay exposed to him, but one end looked scarcely different from the other.

He would not end up under the dictates of noblesse oblige. He had seen too many men and women growing senile over projects of absurdity about which no one really cared: sketches of old houses made just before their destruction, but undated and uncatalogued; restoration plans for cemeteries in which every other tombstone was worn smooth with age and weather. For whom? For what? Ren could have it; his daughters wouldn't. It was part of a kingdom gone, another Camelot decayed because things, somehow, had gone wrong. He didn't care and wouldn't try to perpetuate its memory. He had never waved a banner for it. Its colors all seemed dark.

The minister appeared and Evangeline shifted back, obstructing his view. No clouds had cut across the light against the red-blue panes. Beyond, the mountains would be burning bright, too bright to carry into the soft curvings of the brain. He would have to look away; but now upon the windowpanes floated sheep-like clouds, or were they sheep like clouds?

One day, soon after they moved out, they drove up into the mountains and over a high pass. There on the rounded tundra had moved a herd of sheep that clung to the lichen ground like a cloud. Somewhere there had to be a shepherd, but they did not see one, and John had wondered, since, where that shepherd was. They had stopped the car and gotten out into the stream of wind. The sheep, in a body, had rolled away and left them on the empty apex in the sky. Tundra flowers—white, too, and pink and blue—grew against their feet. Harriet had moved up to him and pushed her face into his chest. He had taken his camera off his shoulder and backed away from her, leaving her swaying. She steadied herself against the wind then walked back to the car alone.

The Bible readings rose and fell, washed toward him and away. Here was this man, dead. He must concentrate on this deadman and on his living family, absorb some of their grief, take part in their loss, but he could not.

The coffin was borne past him. He was still not certain which end was which. Shafts of new light entered the church as the front doors were opened. Cold air touched him slightly. People moved away from him, into and out of light, color. He, too, must leave, go walk beneath the glancing trees, over concrete, over polished stone, up stairs, along halls, through doors, through sounds, words, where people would be waiting, waiting, to look into his face.

PART IV

I

As Ren awakened suddenly in the dark, he sat up. He was
dressed. He had not gone to bed; he had only fallen asleep, fallen
asleep in the day. Now it was night. Traffic sounds came up to him,
working into his brain, blocking the process of remembering. Joanna.
The terrible wall gone up. He must leave, get back to the others, back
to his house, to his work. He never should have left his work to fly off
on this wild trip ended, now, over the sound of buses and taxis, people
rushing. He looked at his watch. Eight o'clock: theater time. Friday
night theater time in New York and he was alone, dressed on his bed,
his club bed, his unreal bed. He ached. He would have to get home,
right away.

Quickly he packed, smoothed his suit, put on his coat and left the
room without a backward glance. Surprising the clerk, he said
goodbye and rushed for the door in an unlikely haste.

He felt a sudden fear that he would be discovered.

At the airport a plane was loading. Ren got on it just before the
doors were closed. Three hours back. By the time he reached the house
they would all be asleep. They would be surprised, very surprised, at
breakfast. He would leave right after breakfast, maybe before, to go to
the office. They need not even know he was back, not until later. By
then he would know what to say to them. Perhaps they wouldn't ask,
wouldn't care. The girls would be busy with their weekend plans. That
was just it. They were all busy, didn't need him. No one needed him.
Someone must. Who? Were they really all gone, dead, away,
destroyed? The work still needed him, the work for Sand Creek. No
matter how he had felt about it before, he must return to it now with
enthusiasm. He could push it through. The prodding, the cajoling,

were not something he would enjoy, but he would do it. Sand Creek would have a center; Sand Creek would have a nucleus, because he had come from far away to make it possible.

Someday his work would mean something, perhaps not to his children, but to the children of others. That was how it should be— his abilities spent for those who lived beyond his acquaintanceship. He would never know their appreciation, but appreciation was not in the bargain. His family had spent too many years, too much effort, working for the preservation of their own. They had denied a debt to those beyond their own. Maybe their selfishness had caused his present position, his role. He now had to look beyond his own; he had to give without expectation of return. Since the death of his brother he was the last male of his line; he must not let the family die in utter waste. That fear, if nothing else, must motivate him through whatever might lie ahead.

He closed his eyes and opened up a picture of a mountain marsh where mariposalilies blew with the fragility of insects' wings. He had a debt, and there was time, or might be. He must not be distracted, no matter who came to him, or what. The petals bowed almost to the ground, and dragonflies were on them. There was the moistness of a kiss. He reached to where it was—full of water song.

A hand brushed across him and he tightened.

"Excuse me, sir, I was wondering if I might see that newspaper on the other side of you?"

That was what it was all about—newspapers—and the shrinking of events, of lives, into so many column inches. At the *Times* worked drones who day by day wrote obituaries for those who still worked and hoped and dreamed and planned what they would do. Ren shivered as he handed over the newspaper and closed his eyes again. The plane was cold, the night was cold, and winter was over everything.

II

At six-thirty he was awake, pink light through his room. He washed, dressed in old clothes, and quietly worked his way through the still house to the garage. He picked the Chevy—the car that would make the least noise in getting started—and slid onto the burning cold seat.

72

On the drive to the Federal Communications Center every tree seemed charged with light and color. The dawn washed against the front range and trickled down the foothills into the valley. There had never been a better morning for a new start. The Federal Center gleamed, its sandstone pink as the sun. The parking lot was empty. Two deer grazed by its furthest edge. The yellow mountain grass moved like a sea, and a jay winged out of a pine tree, calling.

His footsteps echoed through the courtyard. The sound of his key in the front door seemed shattering, but nothing stirred and he entered the building unobserved.

His desk was almost as empty as the day he left. A few notes from his secretary were neatly tucked under the telephone. None of them was important.

He got up from his desk and went to the floor-length window looking down the mesa over the town and the plains beyond. It was all for them—what he did here in the Federal Center and what he did to establish their Municipal Center. They were still asleep, alone and in each other's arms. They dreamed and they tossed. They were people. He tried to picture them. Harriet appeared, her back to him, and he looked away in another direction. She appeared again. There were all those others—faceless but with equal needs. He would work for them though it took the rest of his years, the rest of his strength which cannot be measured in years.

The sun came high, filling the last of the crevices of darkness. It would be a clear day, an energetic day. He was glad he had come back to it. A heaviness crept up the back of his head. Work. He must work very hard today. Every day. There was something trying to pull him down. He must work hard, very hard. He must set his mind and eyes straight ahead over these strands of houses and think of them and their faceless children needing, needing in their worded and unworded ways—all these children of the wind.

The phone rang. It was Benj Southard, the Mayor. That awful man trying to run the town like something out of frontier days. He had tried to get hold of him yesterday, Benj said, about the meeting with the man from Washington who had come in regard to funding the proposed project—"that center thing," Benj called it. It didn't look hopeful, Benj said. It all looked pretty vague to him—the man from Washington. There were no plans yet. Ren ought to know it didn't look at all hopeful.

Yes, he ought to know. With Southard around to frustrate it, no

73

project could look hopeful. But Southard had come to the end, and he knew it. There were others, and Ren would go to them. Right now. He would reach every councilman by Sunday night, work gently on them at the start. He would pull them around. They could override Southard. Being mayor meant practically nothing since the council had gone into operation several years ago. Southard couldn't survive another election. Even if he did he would have less power than before and would soon be replaced by a city manager, a professional. By then the zoning board and the planning commissioner—John Thayer—would have far greater power. They would run the town as it should be run, for the good of those who lived there.

If only John could grow. If only he could carry Harriet—no matter what happened—and carry his job, too. If only he could, he would have this town, he would have anything he wanted. But John seemed not to know, perhaps not to care. He had fallen into the abyss of a job being merely a job. He did not have the self-esteem to push for more, either for himself or for others. There was no one to push for him. He would stay there, unable to climb out. Southard would stay on top of him—Southard, the atavistic frontiersman. But after Southard there would be someone else. John wanted to be sat on; there was no way to help him. John would not get up to scan the larger view.

Ren flipped through the phone book and dialed the number of the Courier. Old Clyde Hansen would already be at work, one of the few. There was something between Hansen, the long-time newspaperman, and Southard; they had grown up together in this town, immigrant and non-immigrant, both pushing for a place. Hansen wanted to unseat Southard; it was no secret. After Hansen would come the councilmen. None of them would be up yet; and several of them would be skiing all the weekend. It might take weeks before he could get to all of them, but he would.

In the meantime there would be this office to run, too. The festival coming up in Russia would take some time. There would be a stream of visitors, the clatter and confusion of the translators, the lights pulsating on telephones. The children. Joanna. No, he must not think of that, only of his work.

Hansen answered and said he would be glad to see Ren. Ren was welcome to drop by his office any time that day; he would be there the whole time, working on a special supplement for next week.

He would go right away, Ren decided. He would not waste a

moment. There was a great deal to fit into this weekend. He put the notes back under the telephone, swept his hand over the smooth empty desk and got up, carefully pushing in his chair. It looked as if he hadn't been there. Again, the fear of discovery. The heaviness. The tiredness. He took one more look at the town, filled now with sun like a lake of light. They would all be awake, up, except for the last of lovers, the most tired of children, His children. Nan and Ellen would be awake and getting ready to go out. He would just stop by the house to say good morning to them before they went off skating, or skiing, whatever it was they were going to do today. He should know. He should be taking them, even if they didn't need him to, as they scarcely ever did. He'd ask them if he could go with them. Maybe they would say yes.

The road down the mesa was almost too bright to drive. Patches of snow burned into his retina, leaving dark spots across his view. Outside his house he cupped his hands over his face, waiting for the spots to disappear. They came like worlds within a universe and would not go away. Suddenly he heard, "Daddy! Daddy!" It was Nan, still dressed in a bathrobe.

"We heard you come back last night and didn't know where you'd gone this morning. Are you all right, Daddy?"

"Why sweeties, of course I'm all right. I had some work at the office I wanted to get at right away. I shouldn't have gone off so suddenly. Are all of you all right?" They didn't know, really, where he had gone or why. He might have gone to New York for anything. They might have been concerned. He might have worried them. "You weren't worried, were you?"

"Well, not really. But you don't usually just go off like that. We wondered, that was all."

They reached the porch. As he crossed the threshold the house seemed to go dark. "Where's Ellen? What are you girls up to today?"

"She's still asleep. We were up late last night talking. You know Frannie Metcalf, that friend of Harriet Thayer's? Well, she called up last night about eight about Harriet, saying she was in a terrible way. Harriet went over to her house and cried and cried. Finally John came and got her, and they decided she would have to get away and get a rest. She couldn't keep on like that, and it's bad for the baby. Anyway, we were up talking about it last night. But we didn't come down when we heard you. Oh. We're going skating this morning, have to study for exams this afternoon."

"You've a lot to do, sweetie. I'm sorry you were bothered by this."

"Oh that's all right. But it is kind of sad, isn't it?"

"Yes. It's very sad. There's much that's sad. But don't you worry yourself over it, Nansie-Wansie. Let me take you skating. I'd like to."

"All right, Dad. I'll go get Ellen up. That might take a while, though."

Nan started for the stairs. "Oh Dad," she said, looking back, "John called, too, last night. He wanted to talk to you, too. Everybody did, I guess. Oh Dad—how's Joanna? Did you see her?"

"Yes, I saw her. We'll talk about it later, sweetie. You go get Ellen now. I'll take you. Then I have some things to do."

They had called him and had wanted him while he was on that cursed plane, tossing around at thirty-five thousand feet in the midst of dark clouds. John, and that Frannie woman—he had met her once—a pushy sort who would work to get her way into anybody's like if there seemed to be something in it for her. How strange. All about Harriet. What had happened to Harriet? He hadn't been gone long—Thursday night, Friday, Friday night. It hadn't been long. Not much could have happened in that time.

While listening for sounds from upstairs, Ren dialed the Thayers' number, hoping John would answer. He would not know what to say to Harriet. She would not want to speak to him, would not be able to. They had lost language, that gossamer bond that wound throughout his office linking the work of one translator to another. Joanna had lost language. What would he tell her sisters? Had he lost it, too? He must not, when he seemed to be one of the few left who hadn't. At least he could visualize it: tender, made of petals, and hard, like rock—a flower in a mountain. He must not lose it, not now.

John answered, after many rings.

"Ren. Oh, I'm so glad you called. I tried to get you last night, didn't think you'd be back for several days. Look, I'm sorry to trouble you with this—I hate to—but it's Harriet. She seemed to collapse yesterday. Can't figure out why, but she did. They found her wandering through the hospital corridors, asking where the janitor was. 'The father,' she called him. Then she started asking for you. She wasn't making much sense. I'm sorry, Ren. This is all embarrassing, but I thought you should know about it, anyway. She seems to have some sort of fixation. Now, of course, she won't talk to me. No. She's not here right now. Frannie Metcalf took her off for the day.

Look, I don't think she's really in a bad way, just exhausted. That's what the doctor said, anyway. Some sort of delayed trauma. Natural, or at least under these circumstances, he said. He said she ought to get away for a while, so she's going up to the mountains tomorrow. I'm going to take her, then come back. He seemed to think she should be alone for a while. A week, anyway. Cloud Valley, Yes, The Meadows. No. Everything's all right. Jeff's going over to his sitter's for the week. I'll check on him. Yes, maybe Nan could visit him, take him for a walk or something. That'd be awfully nice, Ren. Look, Ren. I'm sorry this happened. I was kind of relieved when I heard you were out of town. Yes. I'll let you know. I'll give you a call. After I get back. Monday, maybe Tuesday. No. There's no change in Margot. I'll let you know.''

Nan came leaping down the stairs. "She'll be right down, Dad. Everything all right?''

"I wish so. I'm glad to see you are, punkin. Tell me about your week. I didn't get to see you much. I want to be with you, you know. As much as a father of a pretty sixteen-year-old could.''

As he listened to her eager talk, a brook, he fixed a smile on his face and concentrated on Harriet. She really had been serious. She needed him, and he had put her aside like a child. Of course she wasn't a child. She was a mother. She had held on to him. In all the falling apart she had held on to him. In spite of everything she held on to him. She was Harriet, soft Harriet about to bloom, whom once he had felt compelled to protect, to champion. Had he been serious, sincere? So often he had not been. He had only played at roles. What had he done for Joanna? For Ally? Even Cara—the silly Cara—he had neatly categorized and set aside forever. Any day she might be dead—Ally's sister—and what would he have done for her? Nothing, like the rest of them. Not Nan, and Ellen. He was looking through them, not seeing them, not any of them, and wondering why he ended up giving himself to a building which he didn't really care about to begin with. It was Harriet, the field, Harriet, the grass that blew, the sky, the clouds, the seasons, and he had pushed her, untouchable, away.

Nan was looking at him. "Dad? Daddy? You all right?''

With an enthusiasm that dazed the girls, Ren took them to the ice-skating rink, watched them skate, then took them down town on errands and then to lunch. He talked with a glitter they had rarely seen and laughed with gusto. They, in turn, told him things they ordinarily wouldn't have. The day grew brighter with each gust of wind, till

suddenly it was mid-afternoon and the mountains cut the sun in two.
It was time to return. Time to study. Time to work. Time to light the
fires. How he missed her then. How cold the dead breath of the day
became. There could never be enough light inside the house, enough
mirrors, enough chandeliers, enough that sparkled. The wind grew
resentful, then fingering for holes, reaching for the inside and for each
of them , its own. And in it, somewhere, Ally blew, married to it, one
with it. What had he done to her? What had he done?

He tried to work. The house was too quiet. To whom could he
talk? The girls must be left to do their work. His project—the
councilmen—no, he had no energy for that. He could call Joanna. He
shouldn't have left her like that, with no conclusion, no plan. Cara?
Again, he did not have the energy. Hansen? He could not start an
intrigue, not now. He suddenly felt incapable of anything. He went
out of the house to walk. The shadows were long, like cold rivers out of
the mountains. His coat was not warm enough. He would have to go
back. He could go to the office. He could call Tracy to see if she could
take some letters. No. He could not do that. The darkness deepened,
and the cold. He started to jog, faster, faster, down the hill, away from
the mountains, the cold pouring out of them like a flood, down
towards the town where the light bloomed in fields. His breath came
hard, painfully. The light ahead blurred. He could not breathe. Had
he really reached the end? Is this what it felt like—the shutting off,
the shutting down, the end? He clutched a fencepost, leaning over it
as if to suck breath from the lawn on the other side. A dog barked,
closer and closer. He would have to move on. Which way? Every way
looked the same. The dog was very close. He turned right, to the
south, and up the block on the other side. The dog dropped back. Ice
came into the air. Snow would fall, secretly in the night. Afterwards
he could start again. By Monday all this week would be past and
buried. There would be few footsteps on the snow, especially up at the
Federal Center, where the clacking of machines, of talk, of all the
endless translation would fall soft into the drifts below the windows.
Small animals and deer would play upon the crust, making language
of their own. He would rejoice.

III

Monday was as he had seen it, with a newness strange for the
earth he knew. The tracks of animals were there, the drifts of snow

78

high against the first-floor windows, reaching to the icicles hanging from the ledges above. The office hallways throbbed with energy, an energy he knew he must feed upon as long as was possible. Tracy waited for him, eager to be on with the day. Everyone was bright, pleasant, anxious to be pleasing as well as efficient. By absorbing their goodwill, he was able to get on with the work. By noon he tired, felt he could not even face the cafeteria with its brave ceruleans and greens, its confident statement of well-being. He said he was not hungry, closed his door, disengaged the phone and sat before his window, blinding himself till all he saw was spots, the whirling components of his inner universe, and listened to their words, their almost-sentences.

"It's so cold. It's dead. It's dead."

Harriet. Harriet, folded in the snow.

Tuesday was worse. He signed three travel permits which were unnecessary, even extravagant. At home he gave Nan and Ellen twice their monthly allowance and told Mrs. McGovern she needed a raise for doing such a good job and keeping everything going so well when he was around so little. He called Joanna, finally, but got not answer. He was just about to try Cara, to ask her to visit Joanna, to help him with Joanna, when Clyde Hansen arrived, late in the evening and hesitant, taking forever, it seemed, to wipe his boots off before he would enter the house.

"I'm very glad you came, Mr. Hansen. I'm sorry I didn't get down to see you Saturday. I meant to. I wanted to very much. I'm glad you came. Come in, sit down. What can I get you to drink?"

Old Clyde crept, out of nervousness more than age, into the living room and up to what appeared a suitable chair, one not too soft, not too plush.

"Nice place, Mr. Hadley. You collect things?"

"I used to, and my wife."

"I think I know why you called, Mr. Hadley. I've been following your work for some time. I can imagine what your problem is, what's holding you up, and I think you ought to know some more about him. I can't do much myself, now. Since I sold out last winter I don't have much these days, just help out and give them advice and work on those supplements which nobody much seems to enjoy. I've always liked a fat paper. Used to be we couldn't have much more'n a couple of pages."

"You say you know why I called?"

"Yes, old Benj. Used to spend a lot of time with him, in the early days, till it got so I couldn't stand being around him. There's something about him that's—that's not very pleasant. But it wasn't that; it was what he did. He wanted power, you see. Right from the beginning, when we were in school together here up on Maple Hill Road, he wanted power. Used to trade, try to put things over. Most of us kids were too dumb to realize what he was doing, but we grew away from him. Then he got serious. It wasn't just schoolkids anymore, you see, it was a whole town. He wanted this town real bad. He'd do anything to get it, you see. Threats, blackmail, anything. Now he's after property. He can't go on with politics, so he wants property. Real bad, Mr. Hadley. He'll do a lot to get it."

"How do you know all this about him, Mr. Hansen?"

"A lifelong interest, you might say. Never could stand the man but can't help being interested in him. I'm a newspaper man, you see, always have been, just the way he's always been a power-grabber. Makes an interesting story."

"But you can't use it."

"No, I can't use it. I thought maybe you could. You ought to know."

"Why?"

"I like what you're doing, or what you want to do, Mr. Hadley. Your Center would mean a lot to the people, and the kids. I never could get to go to a concert or such when I was young. Hardly knew what it meant, or a painting. It's taken me a long time to learn a lot of things. I'd like to see you win."

"Thank you, Mr. Hansen. I appreciate your support. I've worked awfully hard for this project, but I'm getting weary now. I just don't know how much longer I can keep on with it. I'm getting very tired."

"That's what he's waiting for, to tire us all out. He has an amazing kind of energy. A waiting kind. I don't want to see him get us all. I'd like to help you, Mr. Hadley, in any way I can. I have files, information, facts. I'm following him right now. I know all sorts of things about him, and about Evangeline. The things I could tell you about her—"

"But how could I use this information, Mr. Hansen? It sounds rather like a reverse blackmail situation to me. How could I use it?"

"Just let him know that you know a few things. That you wouldn't mind letting a few people know a few things. It would knock him down a peg, perhaps take him off your back. He hates you, you see, or your kind, at least."

"What's my kind, Mr. Hansen?"

"Sensitive, educated, aware. The kind that really threatens him. With you around, he hasn't a chance. Not that he has much of one left, anyway. There aren't many people still willing to support such a man."

"I'm still not sure—"

"I'd like to show you my files, prove to you what I'm talking about. I'm not just an old man talking bitter nonsense. Will you come?"

"Let me think about it, Mr. Hansen. I appreciate your interest very, very much. I need help, but this—Well, let me think about it, call you in a few days."

Clyde got up, dismissed himself and was gone into the sharp white night.

Ren wished he would disappear into it forever, that all of them would disappear, at least temporarily. Would they give him no peace? He had tried hard for all of them and had failed. The least they could do for him now was to leave him alone, alone to forget what he had tried to do for them.

The scent of the snow stayed with him, the cold still playing about his face. It invited him out, urged him out, but he would not go, afraid of how it would pull him, lead him running, out of breath, gasping, drowning, drowning. He would stay in, read, turn on the television, stoke up the fire, collect the newspapers, read the Russian reviews, or the translations of them he had paid no attention to for weeks. The Russian festival. The land of snow. The land of the Ural Mountains. Timber wolves and fairytales. The folktale of the snow child, the child of snow who came to life for the old childless couple, the child of snow who melted in the spring and returned each year with the first of the winter. What did she mean to them, who threw their lives upon her, their Russian lives of snow and loneliness?

The phone rang. John. Harriet was safe at Cloud Valley. He had left her uncrying and calm, thankful to be away, to rest. Thank you, John. What did she mean to him? Him to her? Any of them to one another? It was so hard to tell. They melted and returned, returned and melted. Time rushed on, and the only difference from one season to the next was that they were older, irrevocably older. There would be a time, for each of them, when they could not come back, could not unmelt, could not return from the land of clouds and rain. At least once, before it became too late, each one had to state the bond and make it real.

He would go to Harriet and make it real, make her know that the coming and the going, the melting and the unmelting, had substance, meant something. She needed to know, and he could tell her, tell her before she rolled through more years, wasted more seasons, educated more children. She was a mother who would need to tell her children. His children would need to know, too, and he would tell them before it was too late.

IV

No one seemed surprised the next morning when he announced he was going off that day, "just for a day or so." He wondered if they knew but worked diligently to appear businesslike. He packed as many papers as he could find, mostly those relating to the upcoming Russian festival. He intimated the festival was what he had to attend to; because it was associated with Russia, his household seemed more willing than ever to accept a certain degree of secrecy. None of them was sure exactly what his work entailed. Traveling, diplomacy, a great deal of talk, and a certain mysteriousness they knew to be necessary. The rest was conjecture. Sometimes there was a foreigner for dinner, occasionally for the weekend. There was a extra wine, then, and a certain pomp. They liked it, especially Mrs. McGovern, who was sure to inflate the importance of the guest by scurrying as if their futures depended on her service.

Maybe he had prepared them too well. They hardly seemed to notice as he left the house, Mrs. McGovern at the stove with her back to him and the girls in a jumble of papers and boots on the floor. His going did not disturb them from the least of their tasks. He felt a heaviness as he shut the door, quietly. Had he come to the point where he was nothing more than a thief in his own house, stealing away with a bag full of papers important neither to him nor to anyone else? He started the car as quietly as he could and moved out of the neighborhood cautiously. He hoped he would see no one he knew; if he did he would be tempted to stop and talk, to offer reams of insignificant talk, to make up for something, to apologize. He hunched himself up, as if there was too much of him for the seat of the car.

The mountains, finally, absorbed tension and doubt. As he passed through each cut, its snow piled higher than the car, he gained what seemed like a new vision. The valley expanded below him, opened into the vastness of the plains. At the top of the Divide, the watershed, he paused, watched the earth and streambeds fall away from him on every side with the mystery of gravity. Then he plunged, a swimmer, into the downslope trough, his mind's eye fixed on what lay ahead. His breath came fast, tighter and tighter. He could not stop, nor turn around. He had to move ahead, had to find her, find her. Then his breath would come again. He wouldn't die, not yet; he wouldn't be paralyzed, not yet. He must tell her, and then he would be free. They would all be free.

It was a long way, and already he was tired. There was no one to talk to, no radio station that could vault the barrier of the peaks. Nothing passed him on the road nor in the woods. All was a level whiteness interrupted only by the occasional filigree of small animal tracks. Above, the sky flaunted an impossible blue. He stopped once to take deep breaths until dizziness pressed down upon him. Back on the road he sped faster than he should have, trying to find air. He needed to surface, to break through the blue-white element and find her. Everything would be possible, then, and he could speak. They would be in a new realm, disembodied, cut off from ties and complications. She would understand him, and they would know each other's meaning without words. It would be simple, simple as the endless snow that came and went, always the same and yet always different. Harriet would understand, and they could return whole people. They could work as whole beings, instead of fractions of themselves. Hansen, Joanna, the girls, the building—all of it would make sense and he would know what to do.

At the ski resort the mid-afternoon crowd spilled out of the town and up the mountainside. Colors ran together, myriad in the bright sun. He would never find her. If she saw him first she might run away and he could not pursue. As the only man in a business suit, the only non-skier, he was too obvious. From any avenue, from any cafe table, she might appear, only to flee from him. Anyone would flee from him, for clearly he did not belong.

He seemed never to belong, never to be comfortable, though he made such an effort to make other comfortable, to do what was right by everybody. There were so many people, healthy and bright, pushing past him to their happiness. They seemed to have no cares, only joy in every breath. How could there be so many people so fiercely happy, all tucked away in the middle of the mountains where hardly anything from outside could reach?

After many inquiries he found the way to his inn, a small lodge on a side street up against the mountain. He carried his bag up the narrow stairs and stooped under sharp-angled eaves to his bed tucked into a corner. He threw himself down on it and was almost instantly asleep.

He awoke in the dark with wind slipping around the corner of his bed only a few thicknesses of wood away. In the dark he listened to its rising and its falling and to the creaking and the slamming of the shutters. He listened to his breathing and its rise and fall. Intensity gathered in his groin and he felt a sob climb up his body.

The wind sucked at him, reached for him, pulled him to its rhythm. The logs that kept it out were food to it, as was he. Coyote howls rode upon it, or was it only play upon the wires? It came from off the top of the world, or beyond, and said things he did not want to hear. Again his lungs went taut. He could not answer it or run.

His throat, too, went taut as he picked up the telephone beside his bed, waiting for it to come alive, fearing that it would.

Suddenly she was on the line, sleepy and surprised as he.

"Ren! I thought it must be John—that it must be—"

"I need to see you right away. I'll be right over."

He tried to straighten his clothes but knew he could not. His coat would cover him, the cold, the night. He tore through his bag. What did he need? The papers he had collected from all over his house and his office spilled out upon the floor, moving away towards the corners. Lists, maps, prospectuses, itineraries, translations quivered and died. A bathrobe, extra shirts—the unnecessary trappings—spilled, too. The pink package: Of course, he needed the pink package. He would open it up and make her look through the crescent moons and the stars. There would be real moonlight, tonight, to thread through the lace. She would understand, and the moon would become real.

She was waiting for him in the lobby, dressed in heavy clothes. In spite of their bulk, she was prettier than he had ever seen her, with high color and bright eyes. She had emerged from the inbetweenness and everything about her was definite—not beautiful, but definite.

"What is this all about?" she asked. "Is it Margot, and John sent you because he wouldn't do it himself?" A sharpness had come into her voice, too.

"I'm taking you somewhere. I didn't before. I didn't know. I didn't—"

He grabbed her hand, pulled her out to the car and pushed her in. Silently he got in himself, started the engine and jumped the car out of the crusted snow. After several wrong turns and back-trackings all in silence, he found the main road. He pulled up at the first large

84

motel.

"I don't know what you think you're doing," she called out as he ran toward the office. "I think you've lost your mind."

He did not look back.

When he returned, she said it again, slowly.

"Listen, Harriet. I've something to explain. You've got to listen to me."

He scooped her up and carried her to a near-by door, thrusting the key into the lock without a fumble.

"You can't, Ren. You're crazy. You don't know what you're doing. I want to leave. Right now."

Smelling the dank motel air, Ren, too, wanted to cry. Gone was the air of wind and snow and pine which fed his imaginings.

He forced her inside onto the bed.

"It's been awful for you and me. Both of us, and I didn't understand. I know what it's like now and I want—"

She stopped struggling and became calm, her voice deep. "Not back to that, Ren. That was a long time ago. I didn't know what I was doing. I guess I was the crazy one then. Now you. I'm back together now and I couldn't. I couldn't." She laid her head against his chest. They were both silent.

"I've been alone a long time," he said finally. "I thought I'd gotten used to it. But I haven't. Suddenly I saw what it was to be alone and everything fell apart. Ever since that day I've thought of you. I want you, Harriet."

"I wanted you, too, Ren. You can't imagine how much. But it was because of something else. Panic, I suppose. I thought of suicide. Every violent and dramatic escape. I would have run away with you, done anything. I lived a fantasy, for days. Then I clung to Margot's doctor. I even parked outside his house one night and watched until the lights went out."

"And John?"

"He's preoccupied. I don't think he worries about such things. For him every day is X-number of projects that have to be completed no matter what. Oh, he worries, yes. But he doesn't fall into a terrible blackness and wonder if he should kill himself. Do you?"

"I think I've just begun to. Couldn't you love me, now? I see you. I see you and I love you. I think I see a great many things—how we're in a play within a play, wasting time. I woke up in a room with wind all around it and wanted you. If I could take you there, I think you'd understand. We've got to understand.''

"I don't think it matters where we are.''

"Don't make me beg.'' He lowered her onto the bed, slipping his hand between the middle two buttons of her coat.

Gently she pulled it back and slid out from under him.

"I'd like to go back now.''

"You won't try, Harriet, even try, to listen to me, to understand? It's very complicated, I know. Many people are involved. They're all dying around us and they're part of us. We have to say something, and understand. I went to New York. I came back. I tried to work. I saw Joanna. Hansen, Clyde Hansen, came and told me some things I didn't want to know. I wanted them all to go away. I had to find you. Look, just listen to me for a little while. Maybe it will make sense. All this snow, and we're part of it. We come with it and go with it. Do you ever think of that?''

"Yes, but what does that have to do with us? This doesn't make any sense, Ren. You've got to take me back. Right now. Please.''

"All right, let's go.''

He put his head in his hands, unable to get up.

"Please.''

Footsteps sounded over him and water in the pipes. The snowy night was far away, the pine trees and the tundra, the owls and coyotes.

Neither said anything on the way back to Harriet's inn. At the entrance she leaned over and kissed him softly on the cheek. Then she was gone.

He packed and left quickly. The sky burned with stars as he climbed over the first pass on the rise to the summit. The sharpness of the night intensified the feeling of fuzziness within himself. He pushed against the walls of sleep growing up around him. At the top, once more, he stopped.

Stars rested on the peaks, and silver washed in billows at his feet.

He walked to the edge of the precipice where the huge sign explained the significance of the place, the continental watershed.

At the bottom lay deep worlds of softness and of silence where even the wind barely entered.

"Avalanche area,'' a small sign proclaimed. The snow would roll around him. As he breathed into it, it would melt and freeze, entombing him. He would lose consciousness before breath. There would be only pressure and the numbing. The marmots would call around him, the tundra flowers stir beneath him, and he would be unaware. Like a gentian caught in early snow, he would be unaware.

He walked a step closer, shrinking into his coat from the wind. Little rivers of snow started from his feet. He watched them meander lazily and finally slow to a stop. He picked up a rock and threw it far our over the hollow of the valley. There was no sound, though he strained against the wind.

Let the wind have him, take him there to its secret place where fast rivers had their birth. Let him be its child, finally, wrapped within its icy womb. Let him be there with the others, finally at peace.

He walked closer to the edge, pushing out one foot to feel for the drop.

"Any trouble here?"

The suddenness of voice behind him almost made him lose his balance.

"No. No, just taking a look."

"Don't see too many out looking at this hour of the night. You're the first in many months. The last was just about to jump over."

"Oh?"

"Yes. Well, if there's no trouble—"

"No. No trouble. But wait. Do you—do you come here often?"

"Couple of times a week. Run the western slope route. Lugging gas." The man pointed to his truck steaming at the roadcut.

Ren walked up to the man, still a black silhouette against the silver of the mountains.

"Are you going down to Sand Creek?" he asked him.

"Eventually."

"Could I go with you?"

"Your car's dead?"

"No. That is—"

"Let me give you a hand with it."

He gave up. Feeling like a child in the process of being found out, Ren climbed into his car. The back of his head burned.

"I guess it's all right now," he said, as the engine obediently started. "Must have gotten overheated on the climb up the pass." Without looking back he waved and moved the car out on to the road, to the long descent down to the bottom and to dawn.

No other human being crossed his view except a horseman who suddenly and mysteriously came out of a burst of mist, almost in front of him, every bit of his ornate tack shining with the new dawn light. Ren jammed on the brakes for him and trembled afterwards. The horseman, loping off, seemed not to notice.

He drove straight to the office and walked in, exhausted. The long empty marble corridors echoed. He was the first to arrive.

When the phone rang, he knew exactly what had happened. It was as clear before him as the image of the lone rider he had met at the foot of the mountains with vapor from his horse clinging to him.

"Ren. I've been trying to get you for a long time. Margot died last night. I thought you should know right off. Harriet will be here in a couple of hours. I know you'll want to call her. You have a way—well, I know you'll help her. I have the arrangements to make." The hollow voice stopped, as if caved in.

"Oh God," was all he could say.

"Thanks, Ren."

The voice was gone before he could latch on to it. He stared with revulsion at the phone in his hand and dropped it quickly. He put his head down on his desk, collapsing under the weight of tiredness. Sunlight crept through the room, eating up the dark corners and licking at the file cabinets.

PART V

I

The house was no longer cold nor acrid. Everything was repaired, replaced, and the same. Too much the same, too right. Harriet slammed the door behind her and sat on the hall chair, the baby on the floor beside her, waving his arms and legs. As the telephone began to ring she got up, opened the door and went out on the porch. She would not answer it, nor listen to it ring. The baby began to wail from his pool of helplessness on the floor. She covered her ears. Her ears had become very sensitive, retaining sounds that whirled about in them for hours. She could not escape those sounds; extra ones were too much to bear.

When the ringing stopped, she went back in and picked up the baby. He, too, stopped, and she stood still in thankfulness for the silence. They all said she should not have silence, but she wanted it and sought it. Without silence her ears would explode, and her mind. They all wanted her to join things, do things, but she could not. It had only been a week, one small sheaf of days and nights and she wanted to remember, remember before months and years washed over her and took it all away, what once had been when she was happy.

Sunlight filled the house. The sun had burned incessantly all the daylight hours of that week, and she had let her gaze follow its beams with the shining particles that rode upon them. With dusk the cold came quickly and the air emptied. She waited for the dawn, for the brightness of the sun, for the hours of yellow and gold and blue. She went to bed early, right after the baby, and slept more soundly than she could have imagined, waiting for the dawn when she went out to walk in the first of the light.

Come away, they said, but she could not. Before, she had gone away, and what had happened? Without her, Margot had weakened, given up; her eyes had shrunk away from the golden aura of hair—all while she had been away. She could not go away again, though there was nothing here that required her presence.

The little boy seemed happy. He had spent so much time with sitters recently he did not seem to need her. John had his work; he gave himself more and more to it, though he could not stand the Mayor. Ren? She would not think of Ren. He had so much. He had no right to trouble her; her stomach tightened. Her friends? She hardly had any, or wanted any. Frannie wanted to control her, do everything for her. Lydia? Lydia was kind, but held such strange beliefs. She did not understand her world, though Lydia was kind. Who else was there? No one whom she really knew, no one whom she cared to know. She wanted silence in the silver light, the light where Margot danced, the light where she danced as a child, where everything was warm. She wanted to look at the pictures, for however long she cared, with no one to interrupt. There was Mother shelling peas under the branches of an enormous tree and a busy doll's house in the garden of tall hollyhocks. There was a spotted spaniel and a cat dressed up in clothes; a rabbit which got eaten by the cat.

John asked her to help him, to get involved in his work but she could not. John would never let her have her pictures. He would not understand. He would make her go to meetings and talk to women like Evangeline.

At dawn the frost and snow burned bright upon the fenceposts. She looked into the prisms of the flakes and found the silver light all shot with color. Sometimes she scooped it up and held it until it melted in her hand. Then her hand burned as if it held a fire, a silver fire, a silver fire without smoke, and she was able to return to the house to begin the day.

Later in the morning she would go out again, walking Jeffrey in his carriage. She would walk blocks and miles, losing count, until she was too tired to go further. In the afternoon she would walk again, though not so far. When John came home, she looked through him, too tired to concentrate on his face or to latch onto his eyes. He didn't seem to care. He was tired, too.

During the next month, February, snow came hard and regularly. She could not leave the house, sometimes for days at a stretch. She paced the house, took long naps, and still went to bed early, right after the baby.

By March John had become sharper with her, pursued her when he came home, forcing her to talk, demanding that she do something; anything, he said, would be all right with him. He didn't care what it was, however silly. He called her through the day to keep after her. She thought she would scream; she wanted to, after each call, but knew the scream would live within her ears, whirling at her when she did not expect it, threatening her, pushing her. There was too much already within her ears that she could not stop, control: the terrible pounding, the scraping, the sighs, the words, the pounding, the car engines starting up, words, scraping. It would not stop. How could she get involved the way John wanted her to?

Frannie finally gave her up, said that if she insisted on being morbid she would have to do it on her own time. Frannie had better things to do, or knew at least what she wanted: a good time. What was in a good time? To Frannie it was flirtation, or worse. Frannie's husband seemed not to mind. Did no husbands mind what it was their wives did?

The several councilmen's wives who had tried to guide her into good works also abandoned her. John said they wouldn't have a friend in town. Harriet said she didn't care. Friends were only people, and people were everywhere. John said she wasn't rational, that she had to get hold of herself, that she should see about some treatment. Harriet said she did not want treatment, that she did not want to be made different. She wanted only to be left along. John said she would make herself so alone there would be only nightmare. The cycle of their endless argument grew fiercer, like the sounds.

John made them call her—all those friends and people she wanted to avoid. He made them call her. Sometimes they hardly knew what to say; their awkwardness came like snakes through the telephone wrapping around her in a silent, slippery way. She felt sick. She did not have the energy to say no but broke engagements at the last minute, or simply did not go. They seldom bothered to call back, to find out why, or to rebuke her. She had only not show up and they would leave her, finally, alone.

She watched the rain being thrown against the windows, in single drops and in waves. She listened to the wind, waiting for it to rise high enough to kill all other sounds.

The fog came down, deep clouds upon the mountains and rose away in wisps. Sometimes there were no mountains for hours at a stretch. Everything stopped with the backyard, with the wires of clotheslines, telephones and power. Soon that, too, would be gone, and she herself. They would be eaten up, nothing left, not even bones. There was no point in continuing. The wet fog licked at her feet, slid under the door and came up her leg, touching her, tasting her. There were not sweaters, coats, enough. It would have her, all of her; and she had always feared things cold and wet: water in its every form. It would have her, finally, and eventually all the rest of them. They would be together in it, raining down on icy oceans. Margot had been so warm, almost feverish in her dancing, in her sparkling, sparkling dance.

With every drop that found its way down the windowpane she grew older, closer to the final time. Was there any architect who could keep it out? They talked so of human values and needs. John's father talked as if he were the greatest humanitarian on earth, when his own son would not speak to him, when his own wife, it seemed, had committed suicide, though no one had ever come out and said it directly. There was no architect, for all their talk, who could protect their human needs. At least John had seen that and had become more practical. Ren, too. He had given it up and gone into communications, though he wanted that silly building so.

But Ren had gone away. He was off almost all the time, she heard, though no one seemed to know exactly where. Every few weeks he would send a postcard; he had shrunk into something that small, but she did not care. He should shrink and leave her alone. Alone. The fog wanted her. She would not leave the house, except to shop, and then she would hurry back and draw the curtains, turn on almost every light. John said it was a tunnel but lead nowhere, unlike those of the prairie dogs which had their several entrances and exits. John said--

"Harriet! Harriet Thayer! Whatever are you doing?"

It was Lydia, Lydia Whitmore bursting in the door, the door that had not been latched, Lydia Whitmore charging at her, right at her, as if she were furious.

"Lydia! I might ask the same. What do you mean by just rushing in here without knocking?"

"But I did knock. I knocked over and over, and I knew you were here because John said—"

"John said? Why is it always 'John said'? Why does he keep sending you all after me? Why can't you just leave me alone? Why?"

"Because it's not healthy. It's terrible. A young thing like you locking yourself up like this. You're burying yourself. Can't you see that? Maybe no one has been blunt with you, my dear, but now it's the time. This can't go on. You're trying to bury yourself with—with the child. You can't. You just can't. You have a husband, a son, more than so many women ever have had. Look at me. My fiance died right after the war, the first war, you know. I never married, never had a child, though I wanted to so badly. They wouldn't let me adopt one, though it's done now by single women. I had n chance. You've had all sorts of chances. Now just stop it, Harriet, and come along. Get your coat. Get Jeffrey. It's not cold out, only wet. Now hurry, for goodness sakes. I'm not going to let you stay here one more minute. I know they think of me as a silly old woman, but I've got some sense left, you know. More than you might realize. Now come along. I'm taking you out. We might be gone for three or four hours, maybe longer. It depends on the fog and how fast we can go. Hurry along, Harriet. All you need is a coat and boots. Yes, definitely boots—ones that won't mind mud.''

Lydia rushed from window to window as she talked, pulling open the curtains, even opening some of the windows to let the wet air come in. She yanked off the lights in every room and went through the house again to double check.

"You must be running up a fantastic light bill. Or didn't you ever think about that, you silly goose?''

Lydia put her arm around Harriet and Jeffrey and shook them gently. She laughed. "It doesn't seem to have slowed him, I must say. Maybe he's more plant than person. He's grown enormously, Harriet, You must be very pleased with him.''

Harriet had no words, no breath.

"Well, come along then; I left the car engine running. It will be nice and warm. Not that it's all that cold outside. It really isn't. It's almost spring. Did you know that? It's almost spring. There are new buds and shoots everywhere, if you only look. If you only look, my dear. And the birds—the air is full of them, full of them, more full of birds than I've ever seen before. That's a good omen. A good one.''

Lydia bundled them in the car, slammed the door with authority, climbed in her side and drove off quickly. She drove with assurance though she claimed she was old, though she claimed people referred to her as a silly old woman.

Harriet knew she was not silly. Strange, but no silly. They were safe with her, though there was no telling where she might lead them, what strange involvement she might force upon them. Jeffrey did not care. He fell immediately to sleep.

They were rushing towards the mountains, right into the fog. Could she really see where she was going? They went through wall after wall of cloud, as if through a house of many rooms. The house was very large; it was a mansion. Then the walls fell away; they were coming out on the roof. They were on top of the house looking down, over a rippling white, the white of the ceilings, the white of the walls. They had climbed through stairs to the top.

"It's rather like Japan, don't you think?" Lydia asked. "Of course, I've never been there—not in this life—but I was before. I remember very clearly the clouds upon the cherry trees, the buds upon the bare branches, the white and pink of the blossoms coming through the cloud with nothing but bare branches underneath. It wasn't so very long ago. I'm glad I can remember. I like to remember, don't you?"

Lydia speeded up, made another burst of energy around a curve.

"We're almost there, so don't get impatient, my dear."

"Where is 'there,' if I might ask?" Harriet had been afraid she would not be able to speak at all.

"'There' is Mrs. Tatum's, just ahead. Mrs. Tatum lives in a blue house—the sky-blue color of columbine, you will see. It's a small house set right against the mountainside, but lovely. Especially in early summer when the lilac's out. Lavender against blue, and all the other flowers, daisies, poppies, all the rest—it's lovely. Really lovely. But we couldn't wait till June, my dear. We needed to come right away. She agreed. Right away."

"Why right away? Why at all? Where are you taking me? I think you might at least tell me."

"Right away because you can't spend one more day burying yourself. 'Where' is the only place I think will help right now. According to John you won't go anywhere—no churchman, no doctor, no person of any qualifications. My friend Mrs. Tatum might not have qualifications in the truest sense of the word but she has a talent that you badly need. She can tell you what you are meant to do in this life, what general framework you are to follow."

"Oh Lydia! Not one of those people. I'm not that far gone."

"One never knows how far gone he is. That's the whole point. We should try to find out. Anyway, we're going, and that's all there is to it. Mrs. Tatum is expecting us. There's her house now, right up ahead. See? The blue one, just coming out of that bit of cloud."

The path to the house led over a small creek choked with ice and frozen debris. The foot bridge barely rose above the level of the water and was almost as choked as the streambed. Logs with moss and snow reached like bayonets for their legs.

Clumps of snow and frozen mud obstructed the path on the other side. They held on to rocks as they climbed towards the house. Lydia stopped to catch her breath. Harriet looked up. A jay swooped from a tree on one side of the house to a tree on the other side, then swooped back again, calling. Ground squirrels fled into the higher rocks.

"There seems to be nothing but birds and animals. No neighbors."

"No, no neighbors," Lydia answered slowly, still puffing. "Mrs. Tatum has a busy time, though, with all the knowledge that comes to her swirling about. I forgot to tell you, Harriet. She doesn't know any of us, not even me. She won't listen to names, only knows you by the hour of the appointment she gives you by phone. She refuses to hear a name. You've no need to worry, if that's what you're worried about."

Around the porch hung numerous bird feeders with mats of feathers underneath. Harriet noticed a wing—what must have been a blue wing—lying under one. Empty seed shells littered the boards. Chinese wind chimes clattered crazily above their heads.

Harriet struggled against Jeffrey's squirms as Lydia knocked on the door, repeatedly. Harriet hoped there would be no answer, that they could go away without encounter, that she would not have to hear some stranger tell her what she should do when she herself did not know, when no one could know, and when it was all so insane. Drops of water from high pine trees fell on them, wind notes poured over them, and jays squabbled. The noise circled through her head. She saw bells with wings, blue spruce dripping blood upon the snow. Lydia, unperturbed, waited patiently.

After what seemed to Harriet many minutes, the door opened and they entered, without greeting, into the sky-blue house. They walked through several dark rooms until they reached a kitchen, a most ordinary kitchen, it seemed to Harriet. There, over old linoleum, stood a large wooden table which dominated the room. They went to it and sat around it on hard wooden chairs.

Their hostess, Mrs. Tatum, looked directly at them for the first time. The ugliness of the woman startled Harriet. Her huge nose and ears weighted down her face, in folds, into the collar of her dress. It was an endless face. Under the large crescents of cheap lace the face might continue down to the hanging breasts, or lower. Its tongue might lick along the floor, seeking that knowledge of which Lydia spoke. Harriet tightened her hold on Jeffrey, but Jeffrey seemed not to mind his surroundings. Jeffrey, indeed, was content.

As Mrs. Tatum drew out a deck of cards, Lydia handed her a bill; it looked like a five, Harriet thought. Then Mrs. Tatum set a piercing gaze on Harriet.

"Cut the cards, please," she said to her in a deep voice.

Startled, Harriet did as she was told.

"There's been a death," she said, her deep voice wavering, as if over a transatlantic cable. "But not the one you think. Your parents. I see your parents. There has been a crime. They disappeared. They will be found, or one, at least. I do not see this clearly. You will have a child. I hear the sound of childrens' voices around you, but it will take you a long time to know your way. You will not know the sounds of children unless you bring yourself to know them. You must make great efforts, for some time. I do not see this clearly."

Mrs. Tatum ran her hands over the cards spread out across the table but did not speak further. She withdrew her hands and let them fall, with her face, into her lap.

Lydia got up and touched Harriet on the shoulder. They went out without looking back while Mrs. Tatum continued staring into her lap. They crept through the dark rooms to the door, then opened it slowly to the day.

The light was thin. Clouds had descended to make an early twilight. They put their hands out to separate the curtains of cloud before them. Their feet reached cautiously down the path and over the slippery bridge. The air was silent, all locked in place like the frozen water. The car was ice, webbed with frost, as if they had been gone an entire winter.

Lydia was the first to speak. "Well, I hope that helped. It's strange, I know, the way she suddenly starts talking and then just as suddenly stops. Sometimes when she stops I ask her questions, but often she's too keep in trance to answer."

"Is that what it is—trance—that gives her the right to say all these silly things?"

"How do you know they're silly, Harriet? You don't."

"All that business about my parents. How could she?"

"They did disappear, didn't they?"

"Yes. At a lake in Canada. Almost six years ago. It was assumed that they drowned. There wasn't any crime! It was awful. Awful of her."

"But we never know. 'Crime' could mean many things. So could 'disappearance,' for another. We never really know, even though we make ourselves believed we do."

"Well I don't believe it."

"You don't have to, my dear. But someday it will begin to make sense. It did with me. It took many, many years. I fought against it very hard. Now people thing I'm silly. How strange it all is. How strange.''

By the time they reached the foot of the mountain, night had come—a wet, thick night full of presences.

II

John knew where she had been. He had undoubtedly put Lydia up to taking her. There was no point in trying to hide or disguise the visit to Mrs. Tatum. He accepted it, or at least maintained it was full of interesting possibilities which no one, for certain, could rule out.

"You should have another baby, Harriet. We should. I think it's the time.''

They had all put their arms up around her and had moved in on to of her. They held her, owned her. She could not resist. There was no point in exhausting herself in some futile debate. She was the only one who didn't know her course. She was mindless, empty. There was nothing in her but the sounds—now the cries of jays added to the pounding, the scraping, the starting up of car engines, the wind, the rain, words, words, words—all circling in an orbit she could not understand.

Why not have a baby? It would fill her, make her less than empty, less than aimless. It would giver her a reason for counting days, making ready for something that was real. She would have it for John, a huge effort for John. That was what that silly woman had said, wasn't it, that she had to make much effort—for some time? She would do it for John. He could not blame her then. None of them could blame her then or accuse her of doing nothing. It would be much more than nothing. Much more. She was suddenly excited by the thought. She wanted to tell someone. There was no one.

III

By the end of May Harriet knew she was pregnant. She sank into a deep relief, knowing that her course was set, at least for some time. She was congratulated and pampered as her news became known. She had nothing more to do, except exist. She could simply swell and sleep, become the slowness of the summer. She could concentrate on what she chose: a dragonfly, a cloud. John left her alone. Even Lydia left her much more to herself. They were all satisfied with what they had done for her and now they could go their own ways.

By the middle of the summer she felt very tired, more tired than she expected or wished. She fell asleep at all hours, especially when in sunlight. John began to prod her again and to make the phone start ringing once more. She could barely drag herself to answer it, finally refused to. The sound of the ringing was no worse than many other sounds. She could absorb it, as well. People at the door were more difficult. She was very careful to lock it. Jeffrey needed to go out more; his needs increased every day, but it was summer and she could have Nan or Ellen come over or one of their friends. She didn't mind them. The girls never bothered her, never probed her, never tried to talk with seriousness to her. They talked, only, of minor, unrelated matters. Sometimes they mentioned their father; she never asked. He was spending a great deal of time in the east. There was a problem, apparently, with the oldest girl, though she did not try to determine what the problem was. Ren was traveling, too, abroad. He was off a great deal. He was tired when he got home and often brought guests. He seemed to have given up interest in the Civic Center, though he still fiddled with papers about it and had occasional talks about it with visitors and phone callers. The girls really didn't know what he planned to do. Harriet did not care. It was easier to have him traveling; she hoped he would stay away. Especially now she would not want to see him. She didn't care. She did not like his postcards and threw them out immediately.

It was hard to care about anything. They would all make her decisions for her. It was enough to watch it be worked out for her. Every day she was larger, tighter. She was absorbing everything around her—grass, trees, sky. She was, in turn, being absorbed. It was hard to remember what she was and what she wasn't: a woman, no longer a girl; a mother, no longer a daughter; a wife, not a lover; a person with responsibilities, not a creature of the outdoor elements.

The sounds confused her, led her on to the process of absorption she could not stop. Shovels scraping, birds crying, her mother calling, she herself calling—the world of noise orbited her mind allowing her no season of peace.

One afternoon as a thunderstorm collected over the mountains, John came home—long before usual.

"I've had one threat too many from him," he said. "I've changed my mind. I'll work for that Civic Center of Ren's. I'll give it all I can. If it works, it will be the end of that man. I want to get rid of him. I want to destroy him more than anything I've ever wanted before."

"It seems like a strange motive," Harriet said, but it did not matter to her what John's motives were or what he did.

"I don't care about motives. I guess I've never had enough. Maybe this had to happen to me so that I would have some. Anyway, I'll work for this thing. If the referendum is passed in November, it'll go through, and that will be the end of Benj. All of them."

With his mind made up and his decision spelled out, John left as suddenly as he had come. She would never really know what had caused his outburst but she would not think about it. She would not be drawn into it.

When John came home late that night he seemed calm and talked of other things. Then gradually he brought the conversation to her, circling closer and closer to her, a hawk over prey. She must do something, he said. Just because she was pregnant was no excuse for her to sit about doing nothing. She could help him. She could join one of the groups pushing for the Center; there were several of them and would be more. She could even start one of her own, express herself however she wished. It would be a good thing not only for her but also for everyone in the town. She ought to put her education and ability to work, for everyone.

Harriet walked away, to bed, drawing the covers over her head though it was a hot night not cooled by the storm. John did not come after her. She pretended to be asleep until finally she was. When she woke up later at Jeffrey's crying, John still had not come to her. Maybe he would not push her further.

After tending the baby she walked through the still, dark house. John was not there. He might be outside. He might have returned to the office. He might be anywhere. The air was soft against her, slightly damp with the moisture of night. She went outside. The grass was wet beneath her feet. It had grown high, over her ankles. It felt almost like foam, the soft foam that comes upon summer ponds. She felt it higher up her leg, along her arm. She was in a boat, a peeling rowboat with oarlocks squeaking. Her head was upon her arm, her arm dangling over the side into the water, through lily pads, pulling at waterlilies, pure white waterlilies with small insects upon them, insects advancing over a huge whiteness, a huge smooth whiteness. There was someone in the house. They had sent her out, told her not to come back till suppertime; she could tell the time by the length of the shadows.

"Crime could mean many things." They often sent her out. She nearly always went to the pond, into the boat on the pond, out to the middle, past the banks of logs and turtles and honeysuckle.

A meteor flashed overhead, disappearing behind the black bulk of the mountains. Shivering, she went in and immediately to bed, pulling the sheet up to her ears. The sound of peepers rose to a clamor. The dry rubbing of the oarlocks in the wood made her grimace. A mosquito caught, screaming, in her hair. She swatted at it. Was it here or there? The sound went on; it might be both. There was no one to ask; no one would care. She pulled the sheet up higher, over her head, straining for breath. Summer was a net, pulling her down. The pond was full of dead and rotting things. They did not want her in the house. They did not miss her when she was gone. The mountains were coming towards her, closer all the time. John had gone. She wanted him. There was no one else.

At dawn she woke again and he was beside her. She reached out to him, touched his arm. He rolled away to the edge of the bed. She got up and went out to walk again in the grass. The dew was thicker, colder than in the dark. She bent over to run her hand through it. It was silver, like winter come upon the pond. She held it in her hand and carried it, carefully, back to bed. She put it on the pillow and watched it disappear. "Disappearance could mean . . ." She would love him, make him love her. He would not leave her. She would not let him leave her; she would make him want to have her, hold her. "Disappearance . . . Disappearance . . ."

She pressed her body against his back. She had given him so little and he had been patient. He had really been extraordinarily patient. She pressed harder, molding herself to him. She felt the set of his bones, wanted to get deeper. From beyond their room came a thin noise pulling her away, a noise getting higher and higher: Jeffrey crying, trying to pull himself up out of his crib. Caught, she followed it, her feet cold upon the floor, her arms cold in the early morning air. Jeffrey threw a toy at her, the last he had to hurl, then let himself fall down on his bed screaming. Harriet, too, went loose and sank down by the crib, unable to get up and stop the baby's crying, unable to go back to her bed. John found her there, picked her up, and carried her to bed.

"What am I to do with you?" was all he said, as he put her under the covers and headed for the bathroom.

She stayed there for a long time, until the sun was high and the grass was dry, a molten day arching overhead. Over that blue bridge moved clouds, hours, night, more days. What was he to do? He stayed away must of the time and was quiet when he was at home. He said he was very busy. If the Civic Center didn't go through and bring about the end of Benj he would have to leave Sand Creek; he was already thinking of alternatives. She wanted to ask if he meant to take her, too, but could not. He got out of bed quickly every morning and often came home after she was asleep.

IV

Toward the end of the summer Harriet enrolled in a swimming course for Jeffrey, who was just beginning to walk. As she approached the first meeting a cluster of bikinied mothers and infants rose from the blue pool like a gathering of flowers. There were laughs above the babies' cries and bright splashes into the air, upside-down waterfalls of light. There was a merging of color in the water, a palette submerged. Harriet felt a burst of pleasure, almost of hope, as she walked toward the group; she might belong, Jeffrey might.

The gathering opened up for them, enfolded them at the edge of the pool with its water like blue paint. She eased herself down into it, Jeffrey in her arms. He squealed and she held him tighter. He pulled up in her arms away from the water, his squealing turning to shrieking. He should not be afraid, not yet. She wanted him not to be afraid. She wanted him to swim; she was barely able to. There had been nothing but ponds when she was growing up, ponds full of things floating halfway between the surface and the bottom, ponds that grew cold at night and in the autumn haze. It was cold, cold. She dreaded it—the cold and slime, the thick green that would not let her see through. They had sent her out. Night was coming. She was alone on the thick green mass of cold. Someone had come, down to the edge of the pond, and was reaching. The boat was rocking, tipping. She was falling in, into the green cold that caught her by the legs. She was struggling—on the edge—with the water and with something . . . something . . . She screamed. No, Jeffrey was the one screaming— screaming and screaming and trying to throw himself out of her arms.

She could hold him no longer. Harriet took the child out and sat with him at the edge of the pool watching the others—the mothers suspending their infants over the water, trying to overcome their cries with loud words of encouragement and praise, words rising over them in a crescendo of motherly hopes. She scooped a handful of water out of the guttter running around the inside of the pool and put it on the flagstone. From the middle of the wetness crept a cricket unable to do more than drag itself away, leaving a string of eggs behind as it crawled away in death. Jeffrey watched it, tried to reach it, and when she wouldn't let him have it, he screamed for it and struggled to go after it. Suddenly, Harriet was exhausted. She picked Jeffrey up and left. She never went back.

V

The days grew shorter, the nights colder. An occasional day of fog hovered over the mountains. Sometimes John seemed glad to have her turn to him and touch him; other times he ignored her and pretended to be asleep. He had been too patient too long. She could not expect more, nor could she make much more effort. She was beginning to feel enormous, unable to carry around the bulk she had become, someone else's bulk. It was the time of putting away for winter, of searching for quarters to sleep.

John would not let her sleep. He brought visitors into the house at night to discuss the Civic Center and town affairs. He started receiving calls at late hours as well as visitors.

One night in late September old Mr. Hansen, the local editor, arrived and was still with John long after Harriet had left for bed. All evening as she tiptoed around the periphery of their conversation she heard disturbing phrases—coercion, fraud, manipulation—and watched John grow tense. As she lay in bed she could hear them still, in snatches—words and questions, words and questions—and John becoming angry, excited. A darkness grew in her mind. Crime and disappearance. Disappearance and crime. She slipped into dreams that left her exhausted in the morning.

John would not discuss the visit with her; he said she had been free to listen and participate in it at the time. There was something serious he needed to think about, he said, and he needed to be alone. He might even go away for a weekend, fishing, to think. John was not the kind to carry his problems away with him. Rather, he preferred to let time and circumstances bring solutions to him. She had seen him postpone decisions indefinitely. Apparently this decision—whatever it was—was going to be different. John did pack the following evening, Friday, and drove off towards the mountains.

Harriet lit a fire in the grate and turned on the television, determined to fill the house with light and noise, to calk the emptiness against the night. She checked the locks, wishing they had gotten a new dog. Old Betsy was barely alive, far beyond helping her. She considered waking up Jeffrey in order to have someone she might talk to; but he would only demand her attention. She could focus on nothing; there was no point in trying to read, not even a newspaper. She might call somebody, but it was late. She ran her hand over the telephone, scratching out dust from difficult corners. Once it had rung more than she could bear. Now it was dead. She had killed it. Lydia had been right. They had all been right, but now it was too late. John was into the mountains, being swallowed up by them, and she was alone.

She tried to flick on the magic camera, but no pictures came, only sounds and a cold fear like water spilling over her.

VI

John drove quickly, the radio going at a high volume, until he reached the friend's cottage where he sometimes went to fish. Without bothering to unpack the car, he went in and lay down on the nearest bed. Dampness flowed around him as he put his head into the pillow. The waving white line of the mountain road twisted before him, rising convulsively toward his eyes. He got up, walked through the small house, picking up and putting down old newspapers by the fireplace and magazines on the tables. He watched a mouse skid across the kitchen floor and disappear under the refrigerator. He turned on the television, which was only a jangle of conflicting waves, and finally the radio, through which songs flowed from New Orleans and Salt Lake City, Tulsa and Dallas. "I'm a lineman for the county ..." He **got a beer out of the refrigerator and sat down again on the bed he had** got a beer out of the refrigerator and sat down again on the bed he had chosen. The dampness popped up at him again. It was full of the earth below the little house; there was no basement. The mouse returned, fighting for traction on the linoleum floor. An owl hooted and a quick wind shivered through the tall cottonwood trees outside the house along the bank of the creek. He could barely detect the rippling of the water, the bubbling over mossy stones that waited for him there.

In the bubbling, in the freshness, would come answers, out of the mountains, out of the snow from the top of the world. It would all sort out where the fish swam, if, indeed they still swam so late in the season. Thank God he was alone. There would be crying, no fear. Harriet would hold a line, if she felt compelled, but looked away if a fish caught hold, frightened, frightened. Why was she so frightened of a caught fish, of the bulging eyes, the thrashing tail, of the water running fast? Why did she fear the things of the earth? He did not know her; he could not reach her. All he could do was keep her from disappearing altogether, from being swallowed up by the things around her that she feared so.

Why did anybody fear whatever it was that he feared? No one knew another person's fear, no one knew his own. No one knew. No one knew. A branch was beating in persistent rhythm on a window-pane.

Benj was a thief. On top of everything else, according to Hansen, Benj was a thief. For as many years as they had been adults, Hansen said, Benj had been working to build an empire for himself out of the unlikely soil of Sand Creek. He had started years ago, before the university was more than a handful of students, before there was a gathering of scientific ability, before there was an influx from the east—all of them who came seeking what stirred in the mountains. Benj had known all along what he could make out of Sand Creek. Quietly, and not so quietly, he had been working at it. By pressuring, threatening, or bribing anyone with zoning control, he had bought, sold, and traded well. None of it was obvious, Hansen claimed, because he had cleverly gotten all his property under the names of others, sometimes his wife, but more often his sister-in-law, cousins, or friends. Hansen claimed he could document much of it—not all, but much. He had wanted John to go with him down to the *Courier* offices to look over his files. John told him he would have to think about it; he was too close to want to get involved.

"It's you he's after now, you know," Hansen had told him. "You're his last chance before the whole thing closes down around him. We'll have a city manager soon, no mayor, and he won't get the same opportunities. You're his last chance. He'll pressure you good."

"Pressure you good." John smiled there on the bed in the semi-dark with a bottle of beer in one hand. They all pressured him pretty good. They all did to one another. It was awful what they did. His smile almost broke into a laugh. He got up and went back to the kitchen, opening the cupboard doors to see what had been left behind from summer camping parties. Special-K and instant coffee, sugar cubes and salt, instant rice and waffle mix and a long line of ants caught forever in a stream of syrup from an unwiped bottle. It was

104

awful what they did. He was right in the middle of it. What was it Benj had said? Something only today about how they could work together as a real team if he, John, could figure out what was really good for him and for all of them. Something about how he, Benj, could smooth John's way if he could only be a little understanding. Just a little. He didn't want to stand in the way of the Civic Center if John were willing to work along with him. Just a bit. Just for a while. Was it a bribe? He had said nothing specific. Benj had a way of setting atmospheres which expanded by themselves and began a life of their own. He seldom said specific things. Perhaps, as old Hansen asserted, he was too crafty. Too crafty. What was he, John Thayer—another old-timer to be swindled? Apparently, Benj thought so. But, on the other hand, he had said nothing specific. Hansen had shown him no documents, not yet. His might be a justifiable animosity, but perhaps nothing more. It could be an old man's quarrel, an old man's last attempt to square things with the world, to gain some sense of justification. It could be anything. John was an outsider, a threat as well as an opportunity. Which side was to win him, use him?

Crumpling old newspapers without further regard for their contents, John started to light a fire but gave up when smoke poured in through the room, pushing him back. He would not struggle in someone else's house. At home, yes, but not here. Home. A strange concept beyond the attempt of anyone to define, no matter how often that definition was attempted. Harriet was there, Harriet in her lumpish sadness, and Jeffrey, too young to know real sadness. Books and artifacts were there, the furniture so eagerly collected, so unsatisfactory in the end. What else? Clothes; small, queer belongings; the dark interiors of disorganized drawers that defied order; things given but not wanted; things wanted but without value or meaning. That was home. That was what drove him away, brought him back. What was it, really? In childhood it had been huge dark rooms with polished things too soft to frighten, too hard to comfort, and his parents coming, going, until there was no place they had not been. Now it was small bright rooms perched upon the dragon tongue of choice.

He opened a window towards the creek and looked out. Fog lay upon the meadows no higher than the backs of grazing animals. He heard dark horses wheeze and shift their large bodies. Water sounds came through like bells ringing down from high cold peaks, carrying with them stones and logs and trout that sought the sea before their winter sleep. He wished he might jump in to be carried, too, along with happy sounds to whatever sea. It was a pleasant thought, no more. There was no getting out, not yet. There was something to resolve. Now. Tonight, tomorrow, before returning to the problems that were home. Harriet would confuse him. She would look at him in that captured way, bringing to bear a stress he could not understand. Would he back up Hansen or would he let himself be sucked into that strange pool the Mayor maintained? A chill reached up across his chest, around his neck, and he quickly shut the windows. Rows of dead flies scattered at the jolt.

In bed, under the covers, he could not get warm. There was no Harriet, nor was there mechanical warmth. The bed felt wet, as if the river had inadvertently run through it then laughed and returned to its banks. He could not turn out the light and be alone in darkness. It was absurd, but he could not do it. He had not been alone, away from Harriet, since January, since— He would get up early and fish. He would take a long walk, cook breakfast, fish some more, maybe take a drive. He would fill up the day, enjoy it, and make himself ready to decide upon things. It would be a beautiful day, once the fog had risen. He flicked a spider off the bedcover and leaned back to drain the bottle of beer. He shivered, put the bottle down, and shook the wetness from his hand. It would be a beautiful day.

At dawn he still felt wet, as if coming out of a pool. There was little light, mostly fog and cloud. The fields, even the trees near the cottage, were hung with it, lost in it, and the sound of the grazing animals had ceased. Only the sound of the creek continued, to affirm that all had not disappeared. He dressed quickly, picked up fishing equipment from the porch and started out into the mist. He pushed at it, rushing, trying to find something—the creek. The creek was there; he could hear it. He stumbled down its bank until he stood at the water, in the water, riffles breaking over his rubber boots. He started upstream, the current pushing him towards the center, the center which was too deep to wade, the center he could only skirt. A ruffle of feathers broke from the tangle of undergrowth at his side. He wondered if he should have brought a gun. It was not the season. What was the season? Cobwebs suspended across the stream caught him. He pushed at them with fury. Logs barred his way and the slipperiness of wet moss was everywhere. He could not see. He could not see. The fish could see, the birds—all but him. A herd of black angus snorted at him as he splashed by. In his splashing moved the fish, with snakes and insects, secure within their world.

He had fallen out of the car, into the gutter, unable to move while the storm tore at everything around him. He had been paralyzed. He had been too late.

Sweat broke out on his forehead and on his legs encased in rubber. He could not move, could not get there, could not see, while everything stirred around him. Sun broke through like sudden swords. He could not see. His rod caught in a tunnel of cottonwood. His feet slipped from under him. His hands reached out to grab cold rocks—sharp rocks rushing at him. He felt the stab—washed granite into flesh—and felt the laughing river at his throat. Its pulse became his own; his blood, its blood. Not yet. He thrust himself up, letting go of all his gear, and half crawled to the nearest bank and up its slippery angles full of mud colder than the water. At the top, on the edge of a fenced meadow, he fell into a heap, too shocked to shiver.

He could not gauge the time. The sun rose higher, and he began to shake. The rays were long and could not warm him. He looked at his hands, more bruised than cut, and undid his boots to empty out the water. As he sat wringing out his heavy socks, he became aware of a commotion up the river. A gaggle of geese, honking, came towards him with determination. Behind them skipped a child, a young girl with glowing hair. Though dressed in bulky clothes she was clearly slim and light, almost gliding over the grass. She smiled as she came to him, a smile more beautiful than any he had ever seen, and passed him by without a word. He stood up to follow her. He must speak to her. He had something very important to say to her, and she to him. He let go of his socks. She was moving quickly and would soon be gone around the many turns of cottonwood. He could not run. The weeds tore at him. A flash of pain went through him, held him transfixed. He had stepped on a prickly plant, a huge prickly plant that would not let him go. She was gone and he would never find her. Margot! Margot! Why couldn't you wait when all the morning is stretched out beneath the mountains? He knelt down above the prickly plant and sobbed thick rasping sounds that held no tears.

He gathered his things from the cottage and left as the last of the mist was dissolving over the tops of the trees. He drove fast, his mind turned off. He would not think. He fiddled with the radio. Static. He looked intensely at cars that passed him. Ranchers, mostly; state police; opccasional out-of-state travelers, several horsemen, steam rising from the horses' flanks; hitchhikers.

At the next town he stopped and went into a cafe, seating himself at the nearest booth. He ordered a large breakfast and tapped impatiently on the plastic water glass until it came—an oval platter of ham, eggs, potatoes, and toast. Anxiously working over the plate, he ate everything on it. There was nothing more he could do and must move on. It was only nine o'clock; he was not expected back until the next day. He could not wander around; he would go back. What did it matter? What did any of it matter?

On the stoop outside a long-haired youth stood up and addressed him. "Going Sand Creek?"

"Yes."

"Like a passenger?"

"Why not?"

"Aren't you going to ask me if I'm a murderer? They usually do."

The young man laughed, and John felt a crack of revulsion and hate break across him. "Not this one," he answered. "Come on and get in if you're coming." After all, who might not be a murderer? This grimy thing could keep him from thinking about that very question.

He went by the name of Fritz—not a real name, he assured John. "They're only accidents," he said of names. "Like us." He laughed. Fritz laughed a good deal, at almost anything. John became uncomfortable though he wished he, too, could laugh. There had been little to laugh at recently—perhaps all of his life.

At the top of the Divide, just before they started the descent toward the plains, Fritz laughed at the tourists standing in the snow peering into the deep holes of dark small valleys.

"I guess they see down there whatever they need to see. Inverted images of UFO's" He laughed again. John shrugged. "Or messages from God, saying all is well."

"What do you do, anyway?" John asked him. "Anything?"

"Graduate student. Isn't everybody?" Fritz laughed again, almost convulsively. John wondered, without energy, if he should be concerned but he could not make himself feel concerned.

"That is, when I want to be, I am," Fritz continued. "It'd be too much all the time. How coulda do anything all the time? It'd kill ya." Fritz pulled out a flute, played a few notes, put it away then sank way down in the seat. "Whata you do, anyway?"

What did he do? He felt as if he were in a boat, rocking gently, almost asleep. There was nowhere to go. There were no shores, no end to the sky. "Not much," he answered. What did any of them do? They paced, cautiously, from one end of the day to the next and waited for night to fall down on them.

He was going to make the Civic Center happen, for just such

people as Fritz, and he was going to be the architect. The vision suddenly flashed through him. But he could not speak of it, mention it, not yet. "Sometimes I take orders, sometimes I give orders," he said instead. "It depends. As you say, you couldn't do the same thing all the time."

They drove on in silence. The morning, taut with brightness, arched above them like a rainbow. Occasionally Fritz would pull out his flute and play a few bars, never a whole melody, though John had the feeling he was perfectly capable of it.

The vision of his role came and went, came and went, like the view of a far shore from a rolling boat. It wasn't clear. He was far from it. He felt no urgency about it, only curiosity. A sense of relaxation, almost warmth, came from the knowledge that it was there, waiting for him to reach it. Eventually he would reach it and then he would know. There was time. The flute, in its erratic phrases, had almost sent him to sleep. He shook himself, suddenly turned on the radio, loud.

"Now, what'd you do that for?" Fritz asked. "Let's listen to the aspen turning gold. Let's listen to the winter coming."

"It's not enough."

"What *do* you mean, not enough?"

"Not enough to keep me awake."

"Who wants to be awake, man?"

"It's about driving this car."

"No sweat. What's the hurry? I'm not in a hurry, are you?"

"No, not really." He wasn't any more. He would float in the desultoriness and not care.

Eventually—he could hardly recall how—they reached Sand Creek at noon. He drove where Fritz directed, to an old house in the dilapidated downtown part of the city. On the porch of Fritz's house a large group waited from him, though none came out to greet him as they pulled up in front. The members of the household watched, languidly, as if at a movie they had seen before. As Fritz got out of the car, slowly, John wanted to follow him, felt almost compelled to follow him, to continue whatever conversation it was they had been having. There was a warmth, a sense of well-being, of not having to cope with things that were difficult. He called out. He could not move his body. Fritz did not hear. He had gone, absorbed into the group on the porch which flowed around him, an ectoplasm. Fritz was gone and the sun beat down hot through the windshield. He had to get away from it, had to move. There were things . . . things . . .

As he turned his key in the lock, Harriet pulled open the front door furiously. "John!" she shouted at him. "Something terrible has happened. Ren has been trying to get you. Old Hansen—the newspaper man, you know. Well, he was killed—or they suspect he was killed—his building burned down, the *Courier*, with him inside. Ren thinks it'll be bad for you—I don't know why. What *is* it, John? Is it dangerous?" Having said it all out quickly, almost in a breath, she hung to the door frame, gasping.

"I don't know. I'd have to think about it. Was Ren really worried? I can't imagine why."

"Yes. He was worried. He's called several times. You'd better call him. He said he has to leave soon on a trip, a long trip. He'll be at home, now, he said."

John picked up the phone as he came in the door. Ren answered after one ring. "I knew Hansen had been going to you the way he started coming to me, and I'm quite sure Southard knows about it. He has his scouts. It looks like murder though it might never be proved. The building was old and dry and pretty far gone by the time anyone got there. I don't know what we should do about it, John—go to the police, or what."

John said he would have to think about it and terminated the conversation. He dropped his bag.

"Where's your fishing gear?" Harriet asked.

"I lost it." There had been a maze, a maze of old and dead cottonwood branches, of cloud and water sounds. "I couldn't go back. I couldn't go back."

There had been music—so many things. The police. It was unthinkable. What would he say to them? How would he unwind the tangle of suspicions? They would smile, wonder at him. It was unthinkable. He would stay where he was, hold to what he knew. He would defeat Benj in his own way, a better way. Like Benj, he would stop at nothing; the vision had come closer. It was sharp like the outline of the mountains on the clearest of days. The building was there before him, made of the mountains, part of the mountains, part of all of them, for all of them. His father. Maybe he could tell his father. He had been trying to reach him. Maybe he would answer, now. Maybe he would even understand. It would fill up huge gaps, the building. It would make sense out of many things. It would stay there for a long time—longer than any of them. Its stone would not be endangered. It would not be a child that had to be guarded from one danger or another. It would not be a worry. It would be there as long as the mountains from which it came. He would build it to last.

"What does Ren want you to do? What does Ren want you to do?" Words chiseled at him

"I don't know. I don't give a damn. Now let me get away from all of this and unpack."

He would have to get to the drawing board before the clarity dimmed, before a fog rolled in from elements beyond his reach. He did not have much time. He would work with Benj and beat him at his own game. The Council would all come around. The referendum would pass with a huge majority. It was in his hands. It was in his hands.

PART VI

I

The plane glided down over the brown level squares of farmland bearing Professor Wainright Thayer, F.A.I.A., to the west.

Extraordinary how it took as much as half an hour to being down one of these jets, yet hardly provided time to prepare for what lay ahead, he though. Would they both come to meet him, and the baby? He tried to remember Harriet but could not. He had seen her, really, very seldom. And John. It was so long since he had seen him—five, six years? He had almost removed him from his conscious mind. Now the boy was back, demanding to be given space and time.

It was after the child died, almost a year ago, that John wrote, asking to be forgiven, He wrote again and again, the most lengthy and subjective letters. He seemed to be struggling up from solipcism, attempting to use his father as a ladder. At first he would not let himself be used. The cut had been too bitter. What John had said, though in youth, had been too cruel and he would have to learn what it was to be alone. The boy's letters, though, became difficult to discard. His persistence, if nothing else, cried out. And persistence was something to be admired; he owed plenty to it himself, breaking through to a career when no one understood why he wished to work at all. He hadn't done badly because he had been dogged. Now this.

Wainright Thayer finally gave in and answered.

As the farmland became city outskirts and buildings began to take shape below him, Thayer smiled with the remembered clash of pride and pleasure. At last his son had come around.

Now they would meet. But where would they begin? With Harriet and the baby—these encumbrances—it would be hard. But then, these encumbrances were John, and John was back.

The engines slowed, the ground moved closer—so brown, so

ordinary, no different from winter in New England. He checked his belonging, closed his briefcase, set back his watch two hours, adjusted his tie, and brushed off the newly-cut suit where crumbs might have fallen.

He debated going to the bathroom to check in a mirror, to make sure his face, his teeth, were clean but it was too late; the plane was landing. He felt his face, wondering how it had changed in these years, how much more pinched and lined it had become; even in youth it had been beak-like and he knew how the students referred to him. It didn't hurt. But John, and John's wife. He was shocked to discover how nervous he was to meet her again, when the shoe should surely be on the other foot.

How horrible the last time had been, that tearful and silly confrontation. She should, at least, have had the gumption to stand up to him. People with no gumption could never add up to much. He was surprised they were still together, especially after the death of the little girl. John had said over and over in those letters—How distraught they had shown him to be!—that he was very worried about her; she had gone into a quiet state of shock. At the funeral she collapsed. She had never been to one before. How extraordinary! How young people were protected now from all the rules of life!

The wheels touched the earth lightly, then bumped, hard. The hangars came flowing up and the moving picture of the other planes with passengers getting on, getting off. He might have walked, suddenly, into a theater and been drawn by the whirling light at the end of the room. He undid the seat belt and pressed his hot palms against the absorbent seat. He wished this were only a part-way stop, that he could get out and wander unknown among a strange crowd without fear of exposure. He would like simply, to look at people he did not know while trying to adjust his thoughts. He had come unprepared and would tread the brink of failure. He needed time; he needed time. His palms would not stop sweating, and now the plane was almost empty. He had never been good at traveling alone; a foil was what he lacked. They had all left him: Marian, John—and both of them quickly, without a chance to prepare, adjust.

A blur of things met him. All seemed hats and scarves and boots—brilliant flashes of winter color but no faces. Then groups began to emerge—students, businessmen, skiers, families, and finally different families, but none that could be his own. He thought perhaps they had not come—something had happened—until, out of the groups he saw John bounding; that tight, constrained gait declared him. Thayer felt himself enveloped, though his son, he well knew, was not even as tall as he. He was pulled away, out of the swimming color, to a quiet place. There Harriet was holding Jeffrey. The child looked immense. And Harriet was large with the one coming. He kissed them both, then tried to take the wriggling child from her. He screamed and Thayer let him go.

"Well, Jeffrey, my young man, I'm glad to see you have a mind of your own. Couldn't be more important."

"My dear," he continued, "I fear I've kept you waiting." To end the inanity of such remarks he pushed them along in the direction of the surging crowd.

They were all swallowed up by the mass of polished stone.

The trip to Sand Creek, twenty miles away, was a series of fragmented thoughts and sentences. Only the child, bouncing everywhere, would impose some sense of relevance. Like sunshine on shards of broken mirror, he turned breakage into patterns. Thayer, pleased by him as he would never have thought possible, held to him as to an anchor. The strangeness of the flat, dry plains speckled with snow swept by, a total disorientation. The naked land rolled defiantly; no houses tried to pin it down or cover it. He looked away. At home the fences, the hedges, the trees that framed the fields would define the land and give promise of another spring, another cycle of life. At home .. At home ... Perhaps he had stayed too long at home. He should not, at seventy-six, feel afraid of unknown land.

John's house displeased him as he knew it would—entirely magazine-like, anywhere suburbia. Only the mountains marching against the windows made it different, and so incredible were they, they might have been painted. He had expected nothing more of the house. John's adolescent bravura had led him to a complete break with his past.

Harriet hastened to make him comfortable, to get him a drink, to make the child quiet, to stop the dog from howling. She really did her best. He looked forward to the hotel and some solitude. He could spend his nights catching up on some reading.

"I don't mind his crawling on me, really. He's the only grandson I have, you know."

Harriet looked away.

"Yes. Well, greetings, Father." John tipped his glass toward him with that same tight, constricted sense of energy imprisoned. "It's been a long time, Father."

"Yes, my boy." He took a sip. At least the boy had sense enough to keep decent scotch, almost more than he could have hoped. Maybe Christmas here wouldn't be so bad after all, in spite of his never having missed Christmas at home. He thought, sadly, of the mistletoe in garlands and the huge fires in almost every room.

"Mrs. Purvey sends her best, John, and your aunt. I fear she's too infirm now to get out here to see you."

"Thank you, Father. Mrs. Purvey, yes. She's been with you some time now, hasn't she?"

"About two decades, I guess. I don't know whether you'd remember any of the others from home. It's been a long time since you were there."

"Yes. Sometimes I miss the autumn colors and the sailing. The beach things. Only reservoirs and lakes here. Harriet misses the gardens. It's hard to grow things here. It's harsh, you know. Lots of wind and hail. And tremendous downpours in the spring and summer. Snow in June and snow in October, though most of it collects up in the mountains."

"You miss the gardening, Harriet?" She seemed alone at the far end of the room, dark against the window.

"Yes, back in Massachusetts I—"

"Oh yes, I'd forgotten you come from there." Some small town, it seemed to him, she was from: Haxton? Weston? Her people were gone, apparently. John said something about that in one of his interminable letters, something mysterious; he could not remember.

II

Out in the kitchen Harriet put together lunch while feeding Jeffrey. Exhaustion bloated her; pains traveled the backs of her legs. The men's talk continued, rising and falling like waves. They had no need for her; this was where she belonged. This was all she could be sure of—the process of feeding. With food everything was predictable. Only one's mistakes of measurement or timing could make it come out wrong. What could she say to him, anyway? John was all he cared about. He needed John. In spite of all these years he needed him. Thank God John had let him back before it was too late. She had always been ready to forgive him.

115

She looked out the window across the roofs to the mountains that cut the mid-day light.

They were all trapped by need.

John had insisted on the new baby. He thought she needed it. She thought he did. They were so hopelessly tangled.

Running across the kitchen to save Jeff from climbing out of his highchair, she tripped over the dog and cursed. They even thought they needed old Betsy and wouldn't let her die, with dignity.

This evening Ren would come. She couldn't avoid it. He and Mr. Thayer had been friends, though a number of years separated them. They usually saw each other when Ren went back. Ren's need. Her need for him. The need of the child, and that of the unborn child, for her. Her need for them. It was a crazy litany.

At least the lunch would be good, and Mr. Thayer could have no complaints. One by one they would get through these days. Christmas in two days, then New Year's. Then the baby. Already it pressed hard on her. It might go wrong. Only day by day. One meal, one plate, at a time.

III

Up in the mountains snow began to fall. The air filled with the hum of muffled storm. The sky closed down, slipping over the mountains like a too-large hat until it sat upon the town.

Out east, on Highway Three, the cattle began to push together, tails to wind. White and black and brown hides merged under a common coat of sleet and snow, becoming an immense ice sculpture. Unheard they lowed. Far away, caught in lightened warm kitchens, ranchers strained their ears against the wind.

The storm roared toward the east, gobbling up the plains. Outside DesMoines a train, bound for Chicago, stopped dead in the night. Its passengers, waking, put their faces to the windows to see nothing but towers of wind-driven snow. The cars began to go cold. Traffic through them ceased as drifts piled up on each connecting platform.

Ren came at six, dripping with the mist.

"It's you, old man," Thayer said as he jumped to his feet with enthusiasm. "I can hardly believe it. The last time we met was at McCallister's party for the museum. Remember? You and—"

Something made him stop. A sense of total disorientation ballooned inside him.

"Yes, Ally and I got drenched when someone turned on the lawn sprinkling system and we were standing right over one of those hidden spigots. What a party!"

"Yes. I saw Monty the other day. I told him I was coming out here and he sent his regards. Said he expects to see you in the spring when you go back. They miss you."

"I try to keep in touch. I get back several times a year. I've only been to New York recently, though; I can't seem to make it to Boston."

"Nonsense, man. I expect you back, for good, any time. People run true to themselves, eventually. I can't imagine how you keep busy out here."

Harriet came in with Jeff, greeted Ren formally, and passed through the living room to get John, delaying in the bedroom. After several minutes they returned, single file and unsmiling.

Ren jumped to his feet. "John! I'm so glad to see you. I understand you've wrought great things in the last month." He turned to the older man. "You know, Wainright, John has done wonders, absolute wonders. He's given himself completely to this Civic Center business and swung over almost everyone who is concerned. And his drawings! Months and months spent on the drawings. They're magnificent. I haven't seen them but hear they are. You'll be proud—as proud as any father could be."

"What's this, my boy?" Thayer asked. "I don't know anything about drawings. I thought you were through with that and totally given to something more—more relevant, I think you say. You were all set to leave architecture to the old people."

"I hadn't told you yet, Father. I wanted it to be a surprise."

"Oh, John, I'm sorry—"

"No, it's all right, Ren. I was going to show him tomorrow, as a matter of fact. It's one reason why I brought him out here. We might as well celebrate tonight. It's a good cause. I can assure you, Father, it's a good cause. And I think you'll be pleased. I've done a lot of thinking. A lot of studying. A lot of drawing. It's still largely in my head. But it's there. The wonderful thing is, it's there—all of it—and I can carry it around with me, the whole thing."

"Well, well," Thayer said, his voice sounding far away and strange to himself. "I can hardly believe it, my boy. The last time we spoke—but that was so long ago—you had such very different things to say. Tell me about it, tell me about it."

The three men pulled together near the fire. Harriet, followed by Jeffrey, returned to the kitchen. Dark curtained the outside. She opened the refrigerator and slammed it, unnecessarily. The talk continued, untouched, oblivious—oblivious of her, of the whining demands of the child, or of the life—sucking demands of the child to come. She went to the goldfish bowl with the small cold tin of food from the refrigerator. The two transparent forms, all eyes and mouth, stared at her with what energy was left to them in the cloudy water. Immobile, helpless, they fixed upon her. Caught and drained, she could only stare back.

"Fishies, fishies!" Jeffrey exclaimed, pulling a chair over to get near them. She wanted him to. She hoped he would reach them, grab them, smash them and take away their endlessly opening mouths. The child chortled, never before so close. He tottered, reaching. The chair began to slide out from under him and he screamed.

"Jeff! No! No!" She had, at last, found her voice. She pulled him—heavy, so heavy already—from his bridgelike perch between chair and table, put the fish food down, forgotten, and returned to the refrigerator. The child cried unattended on the floor while the voices from the living room continued to rise and fall, rise and fall.

"It's remarkable, John. All this energy and thought you've put into it. It makes me think of what I felt like forty years ago—before you were born—when I got my first big project, or near autonomy on a big project. It's wonderful, wonderful—when you grasp this organic sense of architecture, when it becomes alive and isn't just a question of imitative or non-imitative styles, when it's something other than text-book problems. Suddenly it's real, and it's you, and you know what you're all about."

"You make me envious, Wainright. I've always wanted to feel like that about my work—to feel really involved. It's the thing I've always missed most."

"But you're doing your part, Ren," John exhorted. "What you

do—those cultural exchange programs—affects a great many people. Many more than you could ever imagine."

"I tell myself that sometimes. But it's all a little unreal, a little too far away to be something I can reach out and touch. I don't feel I'm important to it. Maybe I'm just getting old, old and afraid."

"Now, as to getting old, my boys. That's a subject to which I can address myself with some degree of authority. It's a thickening process. The shell is growing harder all the time, preparing for the final frailty. The inside pulp becomes inviolable, almost. In short, you continue. You persevere. You go on, without changing. I'm no different."

"Come, now, Father. You're here. But let's not get into that, nor any of this morbid stuff. I'll show you the plans tomorrow. I found a small room in the office basement. It's quiet, though hardly elegant. Ren, you come, too. I have some questions to ask you. You can help."

"Thanks, John. I don't think I can. I've given too much time to this Center. I've got to cut back, do some things I've let slide for quite a while. I'm trying to reorganize the whole office. As a matter of fact, I have some department heads out here from Washington to go over this whole thing with me, to decide if it's worth the effort, and, if so, how it should really be done."

"You really do sound disenchanted—with the Center, and with everything."

"I think I'm just tired. Really tired. I should go away for a while. Perhaps in the spring, after I've been to Boston. If I get there."

"Come and see me, my boy. Come to the Crossing."

As Harriet entered, the men stood up, drew apart, and did not attempt to regroup.

V

The drawings were good. There could be no doubt about it. They showed all the promise he once had seen in John, that only child who was to carry on his work for him and make it all add up to something more than random jobs scattered throughout the New England states.

He would need more time, of course, much more time, on this job and on others, before he became absolutely sure of himself. There were still indecisions. There always would be to a certain point. But the thinking—the thinking, remarkably, was there. He had considered all the needs of the vastly complex workings of such a building—one housing administrative as well as cultural activities for a large and rapidly growing city. He had applied economy and utilitarianism and yet had gone far beyond. The building might be too self-conscious, too deliberately unlike anyone or anything else. The broken periphery was certainly overdone, even for the jagged mountain backdrop. The materials were uncertain, parts of the interior too massive, too bare. There were certainly all these faults. But it was there on paper. And remarkable. Undeniably remarkable.

John must get the contract. He would do what he could to help. The boy could quit his regular job, that worthless planning of the subdivisions. He would send a check, a large check, along with his formal notes as soon as he got back to his office.

Even at seventy-six it wasn't too late to find a new beginning, a new burst of energy. There were so many things yet to be done. So often they had tried to stop him, or at least divert him, all those people who had come into his life, all those who had become, in the end, merely obstructions: Marian, Marian, the doomed Marian who cursed herself with social responsibilities she could not enjoy; John who tried to throw his birthright back at them; his associates; his sister—all of them. They had criticized him, fought with him, tried to frustrate his every move, but they had never been successful; he had. He would now continue to be, right to the end, and who knew about the end?

PART VII

I

The days of the Christmas visit went faster than Harriet had imagined they could. A new energy filled the house. John and his father worked excitedly on the plans of the Center, day and night. The weather sharpened, the mists gone. Even the baby within her kicked with a new force. She should be happy, she told herself.

John was finally out of the months of unspoken despair they had gone through without discussion. The long silent moods were over but replaced by other moods. He talked, but not to her, only at her, as at an audience. He was busy, but not at peace. He was no longer brooding, but frantic. He had lost weight and had the bright darting eyes of a bird. Fear was devouring him, but he would not talk to her. He would not put his hand on her belly and feel the child. At night, as she struggled to get comfortable, he moved away from her—even in his sleep. When she looked at him, he averted his eyes. He had never been so secretive before, so desperate to keep everything within himself.

"You're not responsible," she tried to tell him a hundred different ways. But he would not listen, and fled.

Sometimes she tried to talk to Jeffrey. But, totally a creature of the present, he did not understand. He knew only his need for her. At least Jeffrey expressed his need with howls and tantrums. The rest of them scarcely ever mentioned need, or gave evidence of it, while they were all being devoured by it, quietly devoured by it.

There was only one way to help John, or to reach him—through the Center. Since she had often heard him talk of the important inter-relationship between architect and artist, Harriet decided to form a committee to collect art for the Center. It might work; it was a necessary chance to take.

She had had practically no experience with art. Aside from a few art history courses at college, she knew nothing about it, nothing practical, nothing contemporary. Ren would have helped her, but, of course, asking him was now out of the question. She must not even let him know what she was doing. The art wasn't so very complicated— only local work—and the local artists were delighted to help her, as was practically everybody. Councilmens' wives, policemens' wives, university professors' wives—the wives of everybody—seemed anxious to get involved.

Even Evangeline Southard, the Mayor's wife, called her one day to see if she could help. Evangeline was unattractive—as corpulent as the Mayor and every bit as over-ripe, but she was one of the busiest women in the community. That she would wish to involve herself in Harriet's work of collecting art for a non-existent building seemed extraordinary, especially when her husband was still opposed to the idea. They must all be going mad.

Evangeline was much too difficult to understand. She really did seem to be trying, at least, to be warm, to be trying to become a friend. There was no reason why she should, especially in regard to her husband's position on the Center, which, though mellow now, was still opposed. Evangeline repulsed her, with that awful mole on her fat cheek and her heavy way of moving. Evangeline should be her enemy; but Evangeline looked at her with kind, helpless sort of sadness in her eyes, and Harriet felt they had an understanding. What the understanding was she could not determine.

It stayed with her, part of her, waking with her in the dark, dead part of night when memories become almost physical. It followed her about throughout the day, but still she did not understand it and thought she never would.

They all lived such hypotheses and spoke so little of what was real. Though John was a licensed architect, he could not work as City Planner and as City Architect as well. He would have to give up his job, and then how would they live? What if another architect got the bid after all? Who would choose the plans?

John might well be fired. He had never gotten on well with the Mayor, and now he seemed oblivious to the tensions of their relationship. He probably said anything he felt like saying to him and to the Councilmen as well. John no longer cared. They must be mad.

II

When John's father left, a week after Christmas, much of the enthusiasm departed with him. A relentless urge remained. Again the sky closed down and snow fell heavily. One day it was impossible for John to get to the office. Harriet urged him to return to bed, but he paced the house, checking through each window and repeatedly opening the front door. He wouldn't play with Jeffrey, whining for attention. She began to worry that the baby might start and she would be unable to get to the hospital. Several times she tried the phone to see if it still worked.

At one o'clock it rang.

"Harriet, is John there?" Ren spoke with a deliberate calm.

"Yes, but he's out shoveling. Shall I get him? You sound disturbed, Ren."

"No, don't get him. I wanted to speak to you. I've got to see you about something. Can you meet me at my office tomorrow, about this time?"

"Yes, I—"

"You know where it is?"

"Of course. I'll see you at one."

Ren hadn't wanted to chat. She called the babysitter, put Jeffrey to bed, and sat before the street window. John continued to shovel furiously, determined to get the car out of the garage and be off to the office. The sky was metal gray and the outside silent, a closed box. She shivered and went to bed, burrowing deep into the still tousled covers. The scrape of the shovel reached her and rang piercing through her mind. There was no warmth against such a sound. She cried noiselessly until, exhausted, she fell asleep.

With difficulty she got through the drifts to Ren's office on the mesa overlooking Sand Creek. He was standing by the window when she entered.

"I shouldn't have made you come out on a day like this, Harriet, but I thought it was too important to wait, especially now."

She looked down at her bulging shape no longer disguised by heavy winter clothes. "What is it, Ren? What can be so important?"

He remained at the window, his side to Harriet. In silhouette he looked unusually thin and angular, like an extension of the strange building.

"It's about John and the Center. He just made a deal with

Benj—the Center for a rezoning of Benj's land. John will write a recommendation for it that will put it through with the Zoning Board. Benj will make a fortune. Actually the land is in his sister's name, and brother-in-law's. They don't even live here. It's well covered up. There might not be any suspicion. But I thought you ought to know., He's gone crazy over it. Crazy. He's liable to try anything now with the Council and later with whoever judges this thing, if it ever gets to that point. He's lost perspective and discretion. He could get himself professionally blacklisted.

Harriet was quiet. She walked to his desk and sat down in the swivel chair. "How do you know that's true, any of it?"

"A reliable source."

"You sound like a second-rate reporter. I don't believe it. John may have his faults, but he's not dishonest."

"He wasn't. But he's not the same person. He's somebody else now."

"He's no more schizoid than the rest of us. You've made this up. To poison me. It's a dirty way to get back at me. I never thought you'd be so crass. I thought you were a—a noble sort of person."

"Don't get melodramatic, Harriet. I can't force you to believe me. I am telling you this only because I feel, rather strongly, you should know."

"Well, I don't believe you Ren. Thank you."

Harriet tried to slip from the room. At the door he stopped her. "Try to wake up, can't you? For your own sake?"

She slammed against a man waiting in the anteroom as she rushed toward the elevator. The floor indicator bounced back and forth between lower levels. She pressed against the doors, as if to force them open. Behind her there was silence.

Outside the cold air pushed against her, gave her support. She took deep breaths before getting into the car. Seated, she methodically prepared herself, fastening the seat belt, turning up the heater, plugging in the lighter, turning on the radio, high. Carefully she backed out of the space, negotiated the huge drifts piled up by plows and headed down the mountainside to the town.

Not yet allowing her mind to turn on, she continued to adjust the dials of the dashboard. At the bottom of the hill she turned left, compelled to move toward the center of town. She drove past the Municipal Building, low and ugly, the building their Center would replace. For the first time she saw it, all that John had dreamed: the staggered outline almost as jagged as the silhouette of the mountains and the beautiful efficiency within. In the central court—John said there must be as few corridors as possible; he never wanted to see another corridor—a fountain would play all year under a clear dome. Everything would be accessible, almost transparent. There would be little confusion as to who was responsible for what. Even the art—her art—would be local, like the native sandstone. There would be a minimum of intrusion. John insisted on that. He was right, of course; if was the only way to pay tribute to the spirit of the land. She fought a desire to run in and tell him that she saw it, finally, and now wanted it as much as he. Eventually they would all see it; they would have to.

At the hospital she paused, almost went in, then turned back to the south. Mrs. Eads would want to get home. Jeffrey would be restless. So much needed to be done before the baby. All the work for the Center would have to be put off. She had to organize the clothes, prepare the room, paint if she had the energy. She turned the radio up high and let the noise pour over her like water. She pushed against the traffic, her desire to be home increasing with every block. When she arrived she ran up the front walk, dug the key into the lock and called out merrily as she had never done before.

By six o'clock the house was clean, the kitchen drawers straightened. The washer and dryer hummed, a fire burned, and dinner waited on the stove. She had Jeffrey on her lap, reading to him, when John arrived, red with cold. She went to him and kissed him, breathing in the aseptic scent of the snow. She burrowed into his coat, silent, until the child ran up.

"I'm glad you're home," she said. "Really glad."

He kissed the top of her head. Then they put their arms around each other and swayed in a quiet and enchanted dance.

All that night they silently clung to each other, weaving their shadows together throughout the house. Their muteness was mutually acceptable. Words were no longer necessary. They moved with the sense of awe of those touched by miracle. They made love gently, with a carefulness neither had attempted before.

Towards dawn Harriet's labor began. Quietly she prepared to leave for the hospital. At eight the baby, a boy, was born. By nine she swam in the aura of relief and well-wishing. Everything was just right, too right. She looked for familiar features on the baby but found none. She would have to wait until he grew. John accepted him. Mr. Thayer was delighted.

She could fall into rest, be rest; she need not be anything more. She had done what they wanted her to, what they had told her she must do. Now it was done.

Lydia, kind Lydia, was the first to visit her, after John. She came with a huge pile of packages and plants, more full of bustling energy than Harriet had ever seen her. She congratulated Harriet to an embarrassing degree; Harriet wondered what the woman in the next bed must think, surely that Harriet had suffered years of infertility. But the old woman needed to congratulate, needed to feel part of the experience. It was all right. The experience was big enough to include her. The muscles of her legs, still twitching, had done work enough for many, and she did not mind though suddenly she was tired and wished to sleep.

Her ears began to ring with sounds—hospital sounds, exhaustion, memory; she could hardly tell which was which. It was hard to follow Lydia, her face rocking back and forth, her mouth in constant motion. She was saying things . . . or did Harriet only imagine she was saying things? The sound of crying birds came from between her teeth, flew through the room and out the door. Long-ago voices, too, broke from the old woman's mouth but said nothing she could understand. What were they trying to tell her, the voices, the sounds?

". . . and then Sophy, my cousin, and I . . ."

A bird swayed ferociously from a high blue spruce limb. Shining particles rained down. What were they?

". . . but James said it was ridiculous—two grown women . . ."

Something scraped at the foot of the tree. The bark fell away like level upon level of doors. Inside was light, laughter.

". . . So we never did go through with it, Sophy and I."

They were kissing her at the foot of the tree from where light streamed. They were kissing her, but she could get no closer to the light. They were going away. They were going away. The earth, at the foot of the tree, became damp, cold. She sat up, suddenly, packages falling from the bed.

Lydia was gone. Her roommate, behind drawn white curtains, was quiet. Still the sounds went on. Harriet put her hands to her ears, turning the pillow. She would ask for a sleeping pill and sleep until she could leave and get away from the scratching—the scratching in the tree-earth, the damp, cold tree-earth.

They would not let her sleep. They kept interrupting her—to ask her how she felt, to bring her the baby, the lump of baby who fell asleep at her breast unaware that she was even there, to bring things, to take away things. It was all the same to them. She might as well be dying. Perhaps she was and no one knew and she would suddenly be gone. Then she would be past the sounds and gone into the chill of the earth, which she could not bring herself to think about. She would not have to hold her ears, she would not have to cry, or at least cry silently so that no one would see.

She had to turn from the pillow one day when Evangeline came by. Evangeline looked into her eyes.

"Don't tire yourself, my dear," she said. She reached out one fat hand, ringed with dimples, then withdrew it. She sighed. "Oh my dear," she said, twice, then quickly got up and left, leaving behind a package bright with ribbons.

Harriet played with the ribbons but had no strength to pull them open. The baby did not need more presents, and she was very tired.

One night, hearing a cleaning cart go by, she jumped out of bed to see. It was an old, slow man, not her friend. There was no one there who knew her or who cared. If she walked away they would miss her only as a part of their job equipment. If she died, it would matter less and would be the cleaner way to go. She was very, very tired, but they would not stop interrupting her, or making noise around her, noise that crashed around her like a surf.

Mr. Thayer called. The connection was so bad she could hardly understand him and mumbled in response. Evangeline called, too. What did that woman want, perched, always, on the brink of a statement that never came? She was too tired, she told Evangeline, to go on with the work of the committee; Evangeline would have to take over for her, at least for the time being. Evangeline said she would. Maybe now she would let her rest.

John said she must be well rested, now, and took her home one day. She did not know what day, nor did it matter in the slightest.

At home the numbness of exhaustion set in as the baby cried through the night and the older child relentlessly held on to her by day. Time fell away from her, as did all but the automatic household routine. John came and went; she did not question his hours or his work. Evangeline, thankfully, had stopped pursuing her, and she had no more contact with the women of the art-collecting committee. They became a blur of faces with rapacious hands reaching, reaching. She saw them only on the tops of certain walls, a frieze. Only what was real to her remained, and objects came to her often with a fierce clarity. She could, sometimes, walk right into the sky and be folded into clouds or feel the inside of a rock. She had everything she needed.

When the infant, John Wainright, Jr., was old enough to sleep through the night, it was spring. She awoke to the softness of green, the inebriation of lilac and iris, followed by the delicacy of columbine and lupine. In the mornings she walked barefoot through the grass to absorb the last of the dew. She shrank down into the life of the bumblebee, yellowjackets, spiders, and ants, counted the spots on the back of a ladybug and took satisfaction in knowing their number. With vines she climbed up the back of the mountains. She let her milk spill down on the earth where seeds were germinating and became part of their silent struggle in the ground.

John told her she must busy herself, again, with the Center. It was now well towards becoming a reality. At the time the baby was born he resigned his job. Strangely nothing had changed the way she had feared. They had money though she never inquired of its source.

From that time everything had seemed to go right. The Mayor came around to accept the project, as did the Council members. The referendum passed it with a large margin. Funds were sought and allotted with difficulty. Nothing held up the process. A committee of architects approved by the Council accepted John's plans, for which he charged only a nominal fee. He had few competitors, and no strong ones. He had never thought there would be, nor did anyone seem surprised or embarrassed by the situation—that Sand Creek had drawn no big names. After the judging Wainright Thayer had wired his congratulations and John had held a small party. Harriet had not felt up to attending; no one seemed to mind. The last drawings were now on the board, and the groundbreaking would occur in June. Everything was ready. She could float along the surface of the victory, the happiness. She had only to dip into it where she chose.

Even the art committee became a strange sort of victory. Evangeline almost made a fool out of herself praising Harriet for the work she had started, the work which she, Evangeline, had only now to complete. One would have thought Harriet had done real wonders; she had done almost nothing and she could not understand. Why would Evangeline seek to boost her? Ever since the new baby she had received praise so easily, too easily. She wanted to throw it back at them, undo all that they commended her for. How could she be happy?

John feverishly involved in his plans, was wretched and afraid and would not speak to her. He seemed to flinch, physically, at every sudden movement, every sound of the new baby, as if he were not sure of his surroundings. He said he was keyed up, tired, but John was afraid, and of what she did not know.

Ren had gone, permanently it seemed, though no one seemed to know why nor where. He continued to send brief postcards but his messages became increasingly vague and spiritless. Mrs. McGovern had moved into his house while the girls were still in school; they were to go east for the summer, as they often did. It seemed likely they would not return. Though the house functioned for those still in it, it seemed to be malingering, dying. The lawn, in a dry spring, was not being watered properly, and the garden, which should be full of new bloom, was almost colorless. Even the hedges, always perfect, had grown ragged and hostile with a will of their own.

Harriet wanted to invite him to the groundbreaking ceremonies. After filling a wastebasket with attempts she gave up; she would have him added to the official list, along with the governor, the police chief, and the other mandatories.

She pushed Ren down into one small part of her mind, surrounding him with images as sharp and bright as possible—images of real things, solid things that were immutable. The magic camera sometimes flicked on, but she turned it off quickly. All that—once serene—now rung with sound that spun her mind. She would not hold those pictures to the light. She would not have the light. Mother was not well; someone was at the water's edge, pushing, pushing. The water's scum came up to meet her. She was crying, crying; everything was blurred and cold; she wanted to be warm.

One day a letter came from John's father mentioning that Ren had married and gone abroad. He had much to say about the itinerary—largely Italy and Yugoslavia—but nothing of the marriage.

Harriet read the single page then turned it over again and again, as if expecting something to fall from it. She tore it up and threw it out before John got home. She would tell him some other time. Now there were too many things to discuss.

Once more she threw herself into John's work and the details of the groundbreaking. John, after all, was her husband, her focal point, not Ren, not anyone else. His work was her work, his interests, her interests—she lectured herself.

A great deal had to be done on the phone. Off the phone she cared for the children, ran the house, and fell exhausted to sleep early in the evening. She needed nothing more and knew no dreams, no restlessness at night.

When John came home, very late, he also fell exhausted to sleep. They did not expect love from one another nor seek it. They knew no loneliness, only waves of energy and fatigue.

Occasionally a flower bloomed with extraordinary color, a sky of mare's tails swept overhead, or an unusual roll of thunder tumbled along the horizon. Then, for an instant, her senses burned. Whatever she saw, danced; whatever she heard, reverberated. Rings of color and sound orbited through her, linking and unlinking themselves in ever-changing patterns.

The night before the groundbreaking Harriet drove, alone, to the empty site of the Civic Center—the park adjacent to the Municipal Building—and stood under the tall cottonwoods. Fallen seed pods rustled at her feet, a summer snow. She kicked at them and watched the silky white strands lift into the air. The trees, of course, would all be safe; John had seen to that. Only the lawn would go, transformed into blocks and blocks of sandstone through which they all could walk, winter or summer.

The spidery lines of the blueprints rose before her; she walked inside them and sat down before the fountain. Her sculpture, collected through so many meetings—so many loops of conversation and diplomacy—looked down upon her from lighted niches. The women she had worked with smiled in the shadows. Groups of children—school tours—echoed down the polished floors. She looked into their faces, watched the color of their hair ribbons, sought out the rips on elbows and knees. They would not stop for her but skipped away, grown old, and others came. She could not see their faces. Some were sad, feeling, as if blind, along the walls and doors. No doors opened.

She tugged at the blueprint webs, tried to go in deeper. They would not give. Drops of dew were on her face. John could see, but she could not. She would be, always, on the threshold. Lifting up a hand of wet seed and grass she hurled herself against the night.

The morning of the groundbreaking opened into a clear blue. The air was still, the leaves poised. From the moment she awoke, at dawn, Harriet knew it would be a perfect day. The children smiled when she roused them. Breakfast went smoothly. All would be ready, and right.

They carefully dressed and collected the necessary paraphernalia, from gloves to diapers. They filled the car. They checked and rechecked. They set off as collected as they had ever been.

At the cleared lot in the center of town activity had landed like a flock of birds.

Harriet tightened as she saw the confusion. Only the evening before the lot had been empty, a dream. Now it was snatched out of her mind and given over to these—strangers who could not see, who could not understand. She could not give them faces nor imagine why they were there.

As they parked and went closer, a coldness went through her. No one looked up at her and smiled. No one would help her. She moved closer to John, struggling to keep up with his eager pace. Jeff cried behind them, and she pulled roughly at his hand to make him run to keep alongside her. Finally, when the child stumbled, John picked him up. Not until they reached the dais flanked by ribbons did they stop. Harriet looked down at her scratched shoes. A shadow crossed them. She heard the ribbons ripple. A gloved hand touched her arm and the rim of a hat struck against her own. She did not turn her face. The shadow grew larger, darker, a nightfall over the day.

"Harriet, my dear, step over here for a moment." I was Evangeline with her petite hands and feet flowering from grotesquely fat arms and legs. She hated her. In spite of everything—all Evangeline's attempts—she hated her with an irrational force.

"You and John are in danger, Harriet. They found out."

Evangeline waved her purse in the direction of the multicolored crowd behind them. "They forced Ren to go, you know, put tremendous pressure on him because of John, wanted him to expose John. I understand he's gone for good. Even married, abroad. They're after John, now. It means the end for him. Harriet, I'm—"

Jostled by people on either side, they were forced to separate, one behind the other. Their husbands, simultaneously and wordlessly, came for them. They left without having looked at one another. The crowd stirred and then was still. She saw no familiar faces.

The sun burned down hard during the course of the speeches. Jeffrey figeted and the baby cried. Years seemed to pass as the sun stretched toward its meridian.

Finally the crunch of metal against hard earth shot through the stillness of the heat. Harriet started, clutched the baby, held herself rigid against it. The sound dug down, a drill, into her stomach and riveted her to the earth. She struggled against the memory surging up, desperately clamped concrete images upon it: the number of creases in the aged male neck before her, the line of a feather on a hat, the fluttering action of a single pennant. Still it pushed up, bubbling at the top of her head. It would burst out and drown her. No, no, no. She called to herself, but still it came: Margot dancing on the carpet like a fairy; Margot pleading and rows of hands too far away to grasp, her mother at a window, open mouths, someone at the pond's edge, someone, someone. A crime.

Tears stood in her eyes. Blindly she got up and left, tripping over legs. As she reached the edge of the crowd she looked back, vividly saw the vision of the mausoleum they were erecting. It would eat them all—crunch them up and swallow them—because she and John had wanted it to.

There was applause. Then, in a body, the crowd arose, coming slowly after her.